THE FATEFUL YEARS:
A MENNONITE IN RUSSIA, 1913-1923

By Gerhard Lorenz

Copyright © 1978 Gerhard Lohrenz. Permission to re-publish this work given to Schleitheim Press by Sophie Hynd.

Cover design © 2021 Jadon Dick, of Schleitheim Press.

Formatting and layout by Jadon Dick.

All rights reserved. No portion of this book may be reproduced, stored in a retrieval system, or transmitted in any form or media or by any means, electronic, mechanical, photocopying, recording, or otherwise, without the prior written permission of the publisher. If you would like to use material from the book (other than for review purposes), prior written permission must be obtained by contacting the publisher at *info@schleitheimpress.ca*.

Published by:

www.SchleitheimPress.com

Schleitheim Press is an imprint of

Okanagan Publishing House
1024 Lone Pine Court
Kelowna, BC V1P 1M7
www.okanaganpublishinghouse.ca

Printed in the United States of America

1st Edition, October 2021

10   9   8   7   6   5   4   3   2   1

ISBN: 978-1-990389-01-6

"He who does not know the past has no understanding of the present and no direction for the future."

This remarkable quote from the late Mennonite Brethren leader J.B. Toews sums up the necessity for *The Anabaptist Classics Series*. When we as a people and believing community forget our own shared journey, we rob ourselves of hard-won wisdom and risk repeating painful failures. In a rapidly evolving world, it is imperative that the writings and histories of the past are not left behind in unread tomes gathering dust.

At Schliethiem Press, our mission is *"accessible, relevant literature grounded in Anabaptist principles and Christian faith."* In this series we aim to remember these vibrant texts, and introduce them to a new generation of Anabaptist readers. Form and function may change, but the inward reality of the Christian experience is a constant throughout the ages. The authors may be with the Lord, but thier words are still powerful today.

We welcome you to this volume by Gerhard Lohrenz. We pray it informs of the past, impacts your present, and enlightens your future.

- **J.D. Dick,** Schleithiem Press, Kelowna BC, 2022

ABOUT THE *GERHARD LOHRENZ* PUBLICATION FUND

The *Gerhard Lohrenz Publication Fund* was established by the will of Gerhard Lohrenz in order to promote and assist the publication of manuscripts dealing with Mennonite life. In the will special attention is drawn to *"recollections, autobiographies, and novels dealing with the Mennonite people or with studies of some phase of the history of the Mennonite people."* The broad categories considered by the committee that administers the fund include memoirs, biography, literature, and history. Priority is given to manuscripts coming from within or focusing on the Canadian Mennonite story.

The fund is run through a committee in collaboration with Canadian Mennonite University in Winnepeg, MB. Grants from the fund are available for publication costs, but not for research or writing expenses. In keeping with Gerhard Lohrenz's interest in retaining, or even increasing the original principal of the fund, grant recipients are invited to donate to the fund. To learn more and to donate, please go to: *https://www.cmu.ca/community/resources/glpf*

All profits from the printing of this book are donated to the Gerhard Lohrenz Publication Fund in memory of this amazing man and his lasting impact on the Mennonite community.

CONTENTS

Introduction to the 2022 Edition .... *vii*

Preface to the 1978 Edition .... *ix*

Foreword to the 1978 Edition .... *xi*

Chapter One: ***Call to the Colours*** *1*

Chapter Two: ***Forestry Service*** *15*

Chapter Three: ***Young Folks*** *27*

Chapter Four: ***In a Red Cross Unit*** *35*

Chapter Five: ***Captured by the Enemy*** *41*

Chapter Six: ***A Prisoner in Germany*** *47*

Chapter Seven: ***John Wiens' Story*** *53*

Chapter Eight: ***A Sailor's Death*** *59*

Chapter Nine: ***Jakob Braun Marries*** *61*

Chapter Ten: ***Peter's Bid for Freedom*** *73*

Chapter Eleven: ***Return to the Fatherland*** *81*

Chapter Twelve: **Peter Comes Home** 87

Chapter Thirteen: **Peter At Home** 95

Chapter Fourteen: **Lena Wall** 99

Chapter Fifteen: **The German Occupation** 103

Chapter Sixteen: **Non-Resistance Tested** 113

Chapter Seventeen: **Soul-Searching in the Molotschna** 117

Chapter Eighteen: **The First Bloody Encounter** 121

Chapter Nineteen: **Rescue of Blumenfeld** 127

Chapter Twenty: **Fights Against Machno's Bands** 133

Chapter Twenty-One: **Surrender and Evaluation** 145

Chapter Twenty-Two: **Flight to the Crimea** 151

Chapter Twenty-Three: **Peter's Death** 159

Other Titles from Schleitheim Press 165

About Schleitheim Press 166

INTRODUCTION
TO THE 2022 EDITION

The Russian Mennonite experience continues to loom large in the collective memory of Canadian Mennonites of Polish-Prussian-Russian heritage. Even though the memory of that era is fading in the younger generations, the traumatic events during the Russian era continue to shape Mennonite identity.

(Until the 1920s, Mennonites saw themselves as Russian Mennonite, rather than as Ukrainian Mennonite. Only a few years before the first Mennonites settled in 1789, Russia conquered the area, and the area was referred to as South Russia. The establishment of Ukraine as a separate country has a long and troubled history. One legal landmark that recognized Ukraine was the Treaty of Versailles in 1919, one of the treaties at the end of World War I, a treaty arranged for and guaranteed by the United States, Britain and France.)

In the past few decades, there has been a resurgence in Russian/Ukrainian Mennonite research. In part this research has been driven by the opening up of archival holdings in Ukraine and Russia. Microfilm of many of these records is now available in Mennonite archives in Winnipeg, Abbotsford, and Waterloo. This renewed interest is also driven by a new generation of North American scholars, as well as by scholars in Ukraine.

So, in light of all this reinvigorated scholarly attention to the Russian/Ukrainian Mennonite story, why is it important to republish a Mennonite novel based on the years 1913 to 1923? The answer is that this novel was written by a person who lived through those fateful years and wrote out of his own experiences.

Much of this historical research is based on official records, including government and court documents, village records, and more. This novel provides the reader with the immediacy of everyday life, the raw emotions of agonizing decisions, and the shades of grey within which people had to make life and death decisions.

The novel does not focus on leaders, or on the movers and shakers of church and society, but rather it provides a glimpse into the everyday Russian/Ukrainian Mennonite world from an ordinary young man's perspective. Republishing this novel will keep alive an important first-hand voice in the mix of materials used in reinterpretations of this history.

The main character in the novel is Peter Braun, who grows up in the Molotschna, the largest Mennonite settlement. Peter's experiences include his boyhood in the village, time as a conscientious objector in the forestry service, work as an orderly on a hospital train, and return to his home after the war. He lives through Nester Makhno's reign of terror and faces the agonizing decision to organize Mennonite self-defense units (Selbstschutz). Lohrenz provides the facts related to these events and also the gripping emotions his characters face as they make huge decisions.

This novel is highly informative for young and old, provides amazing detail, and is an important perspective to ten fateful years for Mennonites in Russia/Ukraine.

- **John J. Friesen.** *CMU professor emeritus*
Winnipeg, Manitoba, March 2022

AUTHOR PREFACE
TO THE 1978 EDITION

The first World War broke in 1914. It was a time when along with all Russian citizens of German descent, the Mennonites were subjected to heavy oppression by the government and the Russian society.

The unsuccessful war and the heavy losses in men in 1917 brought about the fall of the Czarist government. By the middle of 1918, various political parties were vying for power. In this civil war, lasting for about four years, blood flowed in streams. The well-to-do and the (once established) were now at the mercy of robbers, murderers and sadists. The rich and beautiful Mennonite villages became the stamping grounds of destructive bands. What had taken more than a century of hard labour to build up was ruined within a few years.

When legal protection for anyone disappeared and ruthless and wicked bands began to torture and molest the Mennonites, our young men banded together into the so-called *Selbstschutz* in order to defend themselves and their loved ones. Their action went contrary to their ageold tradition and caused a great deal of soul-searching.

The destruction and death in the Mennonite villages after the war and the years leading up to this catastrophe are the topic of the following story. It is my hope that this little booklet will help the reader to understand those fateful years a little better. The forestry service was a large and expensive effort to keep our young men in our brotherhood; the service during the war an effort to shoulder some of the burden our country had to bear and the *Selbstschutz* a desperate struggle for survival. It is not my intention to paint the picture in black and white only. Life during those years was far too complicated. It is my aim to present men and women as I saw them and reflect some of the struggles many went through, hoping that the reading of their story will leave the reader better informed and more compassionate.

Author Dedication: I wish to express my grateful thanks to Harold Jantz the editor of the Mennonite Brethren Herald, who read the manuscript, offered valuable suggestions and gave editorial assistance.

- *Gerhard Lohrenz,* 1978

FOREWORD
TO THE 1978 EDITION

Years ago my parents whetted my appetite for my own history by telling us as children the stories they grew up with. Their little village in the southern Ukraine was one of hundreds of Mennonite villages scattered across Mother Russia. Their tightly enclosed world had been rich in love and faith, and family and farms, and though a memorable Lutheran grandmother turned Mennonite slipped into my line, the world they conveyed to us was the world of the Mennonite villages. There was so much about it that was strong, upright, devout - Christian in the best sense. Their world might not have been large, but they filled it to the brim with the best they knew.

A few years ago, I had the opportunity to visit some of the villages in the Ukraine which resembled the village my parents grew up in. Our guide was a man who had already led a number of groups to that area and was to lead many more. Gerhard Lohrenz has become known to a younger generation of Canadian Mennonites as a living link with that chapter of Mennonite history which took place in Russia. In some ways he has become the epitome of that history. To travel with him and revisit some of the places which march through the pages of our story was a rare privilege.

I didn't find it difficult to accept an invitation to read through Dr. Lohrenz's first attempt at an historical novel based on the events the tumultuous years beginning with the First World War and ending with the victory of the Red Army in the Ukraine. The story is more fact than fiction, as any reader will quickly recognize. That makes it all the more poignant and gripping. It is part of a story which needs telling. I hope many of my generation and younger will read it and try to absorb the lessons it tries to teach.

- Harold Jantz, 1978

CHAPTER ONE

CALL TO THE COLOURS

It was the year 1913 and the place the southern Ukraine. In the broad valley of the Molotschna River lay 57 Mennonite villages, each looking like a green oasis in the endless steppe. The red brick roofs of the large houses created a comfortable feeling of warmth.

The village of Margenau was neither the largest nor the most beautiful of the fifty-seven. Among its families at that time was the Jacob Braun family.

Margenau had been founded in 1819 on what had until then been virgin soil. Only off and on had wandering nomads temporarily set up their tents in this area and pastured here their meagre cattle.

The Mennonites had laid out the village in a single straight and wide street. The farmsteads lay on either side of the street and were 210 feet wide and 560 feet deep, an area which came to one *desjatin**. The sides and the back of each homestead were framed with well-kept hedges, the sides mulberry and behind an

---

*A *desjatin* is equal to 2.8 acres or 1.092 hectares.

olive hedge. Along the street stood majestic trees planted nearly a hundred years earlier. These trees were usually either acacias, linden or pear trees. The house was surrounded by sturdy old trees.

Between the house and the street was a fine flower garden, the pride of the housewife and a source of admiration for the passersby. The love of flowers and for symmetry the Mennonite villagers had brought with them from their ancestral home in the Netherlands. Except for the portion needed for the farm operation, the rest of the yard was under fruit trees or in vegetable garden. Everyting was in near-perfect order. The woodwork on the house and barn as well as the fences was periodically painted; the tree stems were whitewashed each spring. This was done not only for appearance's sake but also because it kepts the insects away. The house was large and well arranged and kept in excellent repair. Adjoining the house were the stable and the barn which compared favourably with any model farm in Germany or England. The spacious court yard in front of the yard was always clean and neat.

It was a warm summer day and Mrs. Braun sat on one of the two benches standing on the little platform in front of the house door. She called her eleven-year-old daughter and said to her:

"Anna, run to the Schulze and see whether there is any mail for us!" The *Schulze* was the elected head of the village.

Margenau of course had no post office. The nearest one was in the central village of Gnadenfeld. From there the mail was taken twice weekly to the various villages. The mail carrier was engaged for a year and paid for his services. He drove a team of two horses, though at times, depending on the condition of the road, only one horse was needed. The mail was given to him in bags, one for each village, and the bag was emptied at the village Schulze. The Schulze sorted the mail and put what was addressed to the villagers into a box standing on a bench on a little platform in front of his house door. The cover of this spacious box was fastened with hinges and could easily be lifted.

Now I will have to correct myself. The mail did not always land immediately in the box. If the wife of the Schulze was one of those bold and inquisitive women of which each society has an ample supply, or if there were grown-up daughters in the family, then the mail was likely inspected before it was put into the box. They read every open post card and looked carefully at each sealed letter trying hard to guess who might have written it. Only after such thorough inspection was the mail put into the box and made available to the villagers.

Thus it had always been done. Of course, no one spoke about it, but everybody knew that this was the way things were done.

In Margenau, as in all the other Mennonite villages before the First World War, hardly anything of significance ever happened. Each day was more or less like the other. Since the villagers were not interested in politics - mainly because they knew little of it - and since the empty gossip of the so-called "higher society" was un-known to them, they satisfied their natural curiosity by striving to know all there was to be known about their fellow villagers. Such villages held very few secrets. Not that one might not have wished to keep certain things private, but it seemed practically impossible to do so. From such a point of view, it seemed quite natural that all mail should undergo a careful scrutiny before it was delivered to the rightful owner.

Sometimes this had unexpected results. What might happen was illustrated by the experience of an old German, a non-Mennonite, who lived for a time in the village of Margenau. He repaired watches and did similar work in an attempt to make an honest living. One day he mailed an open postcard to a friend.

He dropped his card into the post box at the front door of the Schulze's residence. In the Russia of that time an open post card required a little less postage than a closed letter and so frugal citizens, if possible, mailed post cards. Of course it went without saying that the family of the Schulze, on opening the post box, would read these cards before they were handed over to the mail carrier. This time too. They learned the old man had written to his friend, "I live here among Mennonites, a rich people but stingy like the dogs." Within a very few days every body in the village knew what the old German had written, though no one was angry with him. It was considered to be a great joke, and even years later people would quote the old man and laugh at his statement.

Anna Braun was asked by her mother to run to the Schulze to see if there was any mail. Barefoot and lightly clad Anna ran most of the way. True enough, in the box she found *Der Botschafter*, the weekly paper the Brauns subscribed to, and quite unexpectedly an impressive, business-like envelope addressed to her brother Peter. Here was something new! Anna rushed home. Her mother too, was excited when she saw the letter, for she knew all too well what was in it. She took the letter and without opening it set it in a prominent place in the kitchen. It would have to wait until Peter came home towards evening.

When Peter saw the letter he was not surprised. For some time he had been expecting it. He was twenty-one years old and would have to appear before a military board. Every male Russian subject during the October of his 21st year had to appear before a board who determined whether he was physically fit to serve in the army.

Peter's letter contained an order to appear on a certain day before the military board in Pology.

Pology was a Russian town about eighty miles from the Molotschna Mennonite settlement. Two days before they went to Pology the young men of the Gnadenfeld *volost*** gathered at their own volost office. There were 31 healthy young men, all called to appear before the military board. The boys got acquainted. The Oberschulze informed them of what had to transpire next. That night they would be placed in private homes in Gnadenfeld. Early the next morning they would leave for Pology and arrive there towards evening. They would spend the night in a hotel and present themselves the morning after to the military authorities.

Peter Braun and his friend Wilhelm Martens, both from Margenau, were placed in a Mennonite home that night. They were received kindly, given a supper and after conversing with their hosts for a while the boys went early to bed. The next morning they would have to get up early too.

The next morning they ate breakfast, thanked their friendly hosts for their hospitality and left for the volost office. Some of the other boys were there already and soon the wagons that had to take them to Pology showed up too.

The Mennonite farmers of southern Russia used their wagons in several ways. Usually the four wheels carried a box about ten feet long, four feet wide and two feet deep. But the box could be removed. The pole holding the front and the back wheels together would be replaced by one about sixteen or eighteen feet long. A broad and sturdy board was placed over the front and the back

---

** A *volost* was an administrative unit in Czarist Russia with a total population between five and fifteen thousand.

wheels, and ladders, about twenty-one feet long and four feet wide, were placed on each side. These ladders stood at an angle of 45 degrees to the board and on top they were joined with chains, thus providing a spacious and light carrier. This carrier was filled with straw and covered with a strong canvas. The canvas was fastened to the side poles and could not wrinkle. It thus provided a soft, clean and quite comfortable seat for a number of persons. Three good horses were hitched before the wagon. The driver was a young farmer whowas rendering this service not for pay but as his duty. The thirty-one boys were placed on two such wagons. The *Oberschulze**** and the secretary of the volost who went with the boys to Pology travelled on a special vehicle, a *droshky*****, much more comfortably than the boys.

The boys were in a happy mood. No sooner had the wagons begun to move then they began to sing. They sang German and Russian folk and nature songs. The verses most of them knew by heart. Later there was a good deal of talking, teasing and joking. They spoke exclusively Low German. Off and on a Russian sentence cropped up, but that was almost accidental. The boys all knew Russian. Their public and high school training had been mainly in that language. Some of them spoke Russian well, others rather stiffly, the way one does when they use a language in the classroom only. But whether they knew Russian well or otherwise, no one dreamed of using anything but Low German.

*** An *Oberschulze* is the elected chairman of a volost, similar to a Reeve or Mayor in North America.

**** A *droshky* is a low four-wheeled open carriage of a kind formerly used in Russia.

Peter Braun and his friend Willy sat close to the rear of the wagon. Both knew they were healthy and likely to be drafted. Their service would last three years and the military board summons was very important to them.

"Suppose you are drafted, Peter," asked Willy. "Will you be very sorry?"

"No," replied Peter. "'In fact I won't mind. My parents keep a weekly Mennonite paper from America which says that serving in the forestry camps is a waste of time. Our young men are losing three precious years, thus the paper asserts. But I don't see it that way. What do they actually mean, losing three years'? Preventing them from farming or engaging in business? Why should men be in such a hurry to engage in some money-making occupation? Is acquiring possessions the highest aim in life? I don't think so. The highest aim should be to live a meaningful life, and I consider the service in a forestry unit to be meaningful. Not in the sense that one acquires property but in living together with other fellows, getting to know many of them and engaging in the give and take of daily life."

"Yes," said Willy. "I think you are right, but still, three years are a long time. Why must the state demand such a long service?"

"The term could possibly be shorter, but other young men of our country have to serve that long in the regular army and even longer in the Navy. We as Mennonites are also Russian citizens and enjoy all the benefits that others do; certainly we should bear the same responsibilities our non-Mennonite fellow citizens do."

"But Peter, why should the young men of our country serve? Why must we have such a large army?'" asked Willy.

"Because we live in a world which can't get along without force. If we lived in paradise we wouldn't need an army, but in the imperfect world in which we live, governments must be able to impose their will upon their own unruly elements. And, as well, jealousy, suspicion and rivalry between various nations. Each government fears to be weak, or weaker than its neighbors. I admit, all of this is the result of human imperfection, but as long as mankind remains what it is, governments will have to have armies."

"But even today there are countries which do not force their young men to serve in the army - take the United States, for instance," objected Willy.

"Well, the United States has an army too. Their soldiers are hired and serve for money. As a nation they do not need an army as large as Russia's simply because the United States has no strong neighbors it fears, while our situation is quite different. Russia is surrounded by strong and ambitious neighbors and must be ready to meet possible threats to its territory."

"I guess you are right," conceded Willy. "But I still think the nations should aim at more sensible relationships with each other, ones that would not be based on costly military establishments."

"That, my dear friend, cannot be disputed," Peter said, closing the topic. "But so far this sensible basis has not been found and until they do, I am afraid armies will exist and you and I will likely have to do our bit in serving old Russia."

Their discussion was interrupted by a youth from another village.

"Braun and Martens," he said, "you Margenauers. We are interested in a story. We have heard that a woman in your village had an extraordinary dream which was later fulfilled. Tell us about it."

"I suppose you are referring to Tante Gerhard Harder," Jacob replied, "Yes, that is a remarkable story. Harder, a farmer in our village, had lost his young wife and then married her girlfriend, Maria Friesen. On the third or fourth night their married life the young Tante Harder had a dream - she thought it was more than a dream. She dreamt that her friend, the first Tante Harder, was standing at her bedside and saying to her, 'Mary, your marriage is not for long. It will last two years only.' Then Mary Harder awoke. She thought about her strange dream but eventually she fell asleep again. Then the dream repeated itself. Again she was told that she had only two years. Now she was badly shaken. She awakened her husband and told him of her dream, and the following day she told it to a number of people. She was convinced that the prediction would come true. And it did too. The Harders were married on March 16, 1905 and Mary became ill and died on March 16, 1907."

This led to a general discussion about dreams and their reliability. There were many opinions but finally the youths agreed that while dreams in general have no meaning, there have always been exceptions - dreams which pass on reliable and important messages to the sleeper. Such dreams, it was agreed, are divinely inspired and must not be taken lightly.

In the late afternoon the youths drove into Pology, one of those sprawling Russian settlements which impress the visitor as a cross between a neglected overgrown village and a city. In such places one finds the greatest contrasts: poor peasant and workers' homes on dusty or muddy streets, depending upon the weather, and modern business establishments on streets laid out with cobblestones. They stopped at an inn, a place where the horses could be stabled and the men could get rooms. The rooms were not too bad. Private washrooms in such a place of course were unheard of but on each floor was a toilet and bathing facility. The rooms could take from four to ten men, giving each a private bed. Meals were available at any time of the day in a nearby restaurant. It was a fairly clean place, had good service and offered good meals. The boys washed up and ate supper. Later on they roamed the streets of Pology. Very seldom had they been out of their quiet villages and even Pology held their interest.

The Oberschulze and his secretary too took a room in the inn. They were in charge of affairs, because the boys, well informed and competent in their villages and on their farms, were on foreign soil in the city and felt quite helpless.

Next morning they went to the place assigned to them, where they found many other young men, Russians, Jews, Bulgarians and others. All had to present themselves for service. Each man had to draw a lot with a number. From the lot, he knew his place in the lineup before the Board. Peter Braun drew a low number, 49. All he had to do now was to wait for his number to be called.

When his number came up Peter entered a room with several busy secretaries. He was assigned to the desk of one of them. The secretary questioned Peter and entered his replies on a sheet. The questions dealt with Peter's family and his own situation. When he was finished Peter was ordered to the next room. Here a Russian officer was in charge. On a bench Peter saw a number of completely naked men sitting. Peter, too, was ordered to undress. His belongings he placed in a small wardrobe. This the man locked after writing down Peter's name and the number of his wardrobe. Then he was asked to take his place on the bench too.

It wasn't long before Peter was called into the adjoining room. Here were three medical doctors and a secretary. The doctors examined him closely: they looked at his eyes, his teeth, his nose and his genitals, listened to his heartbeat and to his breathing, thumped his chest, inspected his feet, and finally pronounced him *"Goden,"* physically well and strong enough to serve in the army.

The young men who did not meet the health requirements were given a paper and sent out as free men. Others, like Peter Braun, were pronounced fit and had to go to another room. Here they presented themselves to another official. This man had all the information about each of the young men. According to law, certain men were freed from all service because of family circumstances. The only son in a family, the son of a widow who relied on him for her livelihood, or a son in some similar situation, were freed from all obligations to the state. They were given a white passport, henceforth their passport would have that colour. The holder of such a passport, though physically fit, was freed from all obligations because of family considerations. Everyone else was obligated to serve. Peter Braun was among the latter group.

But even now there still was a small chance for a young man to escape all service. Annually the state took a set number of young men into the army. Usually there were more available than required. Each man had to draw a lot. Those with the high numbers were freed from all service. Peter was not among the lucky.

All those who would be entering the service now were allowed to go home, but each was told where he had to present himself at the beginning of the new year. The Mennonites would be informed in due time about the forestry unit to which they would have to present themselves. They were not asked for their likes or views. But the privilege granted the *Mennonite brotherhood****** guaranteed that a young man of Mennonite parentage automatically went to one of the forestry units to fulfill his service. Like all Russian citizens he had to serve three years. A man with a superior education served two years only and also enjoyed certain privileges. A man with a teacher's certificate needn't service in the army at all if he was willing to teach in a public school at full pay for five years.

In due time Peter Braun was informed that he had to present himself on the first of March at the Vladimirow Forestry Camp, situated near the Sagradowka Mennonite settlement. He knew that there were altogether eight forestry camps on which about 1,200 men were serving.

Peter was the reflective type. One who liked to analyse things. Until now the whole forestry matter had been of marginal interest to him, but now that he would have to serve on one of these forestry units for three years he became vitally interested in the whole arrangement. He knew that the government decided where each individual had to serve and that men belonging to different conferences thus served side by side. This would not have been possible had the decision rested with the Mennonite brotherhood, he felt. Then there would have been forestry units for the "church" Mennonites and others for the Mennonite Brethren. They could impossibly have served together. Peter was pleased that things were as they were. He looked forward to serving with men of different church backgrounds.

***** The *Mennonite brotherhood* refers to a governing group made up of both Mennonite Conference and Mennonite Brethren leaders.

Young Russians had to serve in the regular army. Peter and others like him gave their service doing physical work, planting trees and looking after forests.

But did this non-participation in the military really flow out of a deep conviction about nonresistance? Peter was not so sure. The principle had never been explained to him and other young men with any depth; it had been mentioned only marginally. And in practical life it did not seem to be too important either. Thus the members of the Mennonite Brethren Church, who were so careful with whom they took communion, quite readily shared the communion table with the Baptists. The Baptists served in the regular army and did not believe in non-resistance. This did not seem to be important enough to serve as a barrier between the non-resisting Mennonites and the resistance-approving Baptists.

But if this was the situation why was the Mennonite brotherhood willing to make the great financial sacrifices demanded by the forestry service? Peter decided it was mainly because of the desire to isolate their sons from too close contacts with other groups. Such contacts would estrange some of the young men from the brotherhood, lead to intermarriages and eventually end in the breakup on their ethnic and religious group in Russia. To prevent this, the brotherhood was willing to make great material sacrifices. This, Peter felt, was not to say that the belief in non-resistance did not matter; it did, but it was not a dominating influence.

CHAPTER TWO

FORESTRY SERVICE

On March 1st, 1913, Peter Braun and 33 other young recruits presented themselves at the Vladimirow forestry camp. It was one of the eight forestry units maintained by the Mennonite brotherhood. Peter knew that this station covered 3,000 desjatins (8,400 acres) and that about 1,900 desjatins of these were forest that had been planted by earlier companies of young Mennonites. The land belonged to the state, but the buildings on it were erected with Mennonite money. There was room for 131 men in service. They were placed in large rooms, ten or twelve to a room. Other rooms held offices, the dining hall and so on.

Peter had a fairly good idea about what awaited. The men already in the camp had known for weeks who the newcomers would be and had gathered on most of them an impressive amount of information. Among the men serving here were some from practically every Mennonite settlement in Russia and this enabled them to collect much information. Thus it had been decided long ago who would receive what reception. If a newcomer was inclined to swagger, or if he was reported to be a boaster, or showed some other socially unacceptable character traits, then he was in for a special treatment. Peter knew that the fellows, bored by the monotonous life in the forestry station, had been waiting impatiently for the arrival of the new bunch.

Most of the recruits had already met on the train or at the railway station. From the station they had engaged a few Russion peasants to drive them to the forestry camp. It was a twenty mile drive. Most of the young men wondered somewhat apprehensively what might be in store for them at the end of the drive. When the teams approached their destination, the newcomers could see a few uniformed men standing around in the yard. Then they heard a shout, and dozens of other uniformed men poured out of the doors. About a hundred men now awaited the newcomers. When the wagons had come to a standstill a mighty shout went up: "Welcome to Vladimir! Welcome, you suckers!"

The men rushed to the wagons and surrounded them and boldly appraised the newcomers. Their exclamations rose: "Aren't they beautiful! Good looking, but hey, there is also an ugly one in the bunch. Look at that giant over there! He does look mean, does he not? All right, fellows. What are you waiting for? Climb down, don't be shy!"

As soon as the boys stood on the ground each was surrounded by several fellows. Peter could hear them ask: "What is your name? How old are you? Have you got sisters and what are their names? Have you gotta girlfriend?" No matter how the newcomer answered, there was always something that the questioners marveled about. If he said that he did not have a girlfriend, they were amazed: "How come," they marveled. "A healthy man like you, good looking and obviously smart, and not to have a girlfriend! How come? Explain!" If on the other hand, the man admitted that he did have a girlfriend, the fellows were equally surprised. "Au, au!" they said. "You seem to be a fast fellow with the girls, are you not? What is the name of your beloved one? What is she like? Does she have a sister?" and so on and on.

There was one fellow among the recruits who had grown up on a *chutor** and preferred to speak Russian. Peter noticed this caused quite a stir. The men seemed to be awed and inquired whether he spoke Russian all the time. When he confirmed that he did, they wanted to know whether this was hard on him: had the skin on his chest not peeled off from such effort? He should show his chest to them. Someone offered to fetch some liniment and to rub his chest; that, they assured the Russian-speaking man, would ease the strain he must be under.

One or two of the newcomers had apparently been reported as being "proud". The men pretended to take them as highly educated and sophisticated persons, and treated them with exaggerated respect. They addressed them not with the common '"you" used by everybody around here but the respectful "thou". In the Low German language these two terms have quite a different meaning. "You" is the term used among close friends or towards younger people, but "thou'" is used towards much older or respected individuals.

On the train Peter's attention had already been drawn to a young, well-dressed man who had kept apart from the group. He had been reading a paper and acted as if he did not care to mingle with the rest. Upon inquiring, Peter was told he was the son of a

---

* A *chutor* was a country estate. It could be small or large, but it was an independent unit and not part of a village.

Mennonite factory owner. The family was very rich. The father was not a bad man, but the son had a very high opinion of himself and despised ordinary Mennonite farmer boys.

Several fellows came up to the millionaire's son. Peter heard them exclaim: "Look here! An oxen, really and truly, an oxen! A stupid one at that. Look at his face! He has a good opinion of himself!"

"But why should he be so proud?" one enquired.

"Out of sheer stupidity," someone explained. Then they said: "Let us take this oxen into the cowshed where he belongs. It's not fitting to leave him here among human beings."

Two men got hold of the foppish young man's arms and dragged him towards the cowshed. Several others folowed, making comments as they walked. In the cowshed they placed the fop in a row with the oxen standing there, and and tied him with a rope and put hay in front of him.

Only then did the fellows seem to become aware that this newcomer spoke with a human voice. "You can speak? Are you human? Oh, a forgive us, forgive us! We took you to be an oxen; and truly you you look every bit like one. But if you are a human being, then you don't belong here. We are sorry!" Then they explained to the young dandy that in the forestry service all men were considered equals and treated as equals. Whatever the family might own was of no interest to them, nor did education make much of an impression. A man was judged here by his conduct, how he treated his fellow labourer. Did he think that he could accept such an attitude and try to live by it? If he did, then they were prepared to take him into the barracks; but if not, then it was best for him to remain where he was, in the cowshed among the oxen. The foppish youth assured the men that he intended to be a good comrade. With this assurance, he was untied and allowed to move into the barracks. Such treatment was given not because this fellow was the son of a rich family, but, as the others explained it, "because he has too many raisins in his head."

Most of the things done this day were harmless in nature, perhaps a little rude, but if the newcomer entered into the spirit of the game he soon was left alone. But if he got angry or showed his displeasure, he made himself the butt of special treatment that he would likely remember for years. Peter did not see anyone physically molested, but in the weeks that followed some individuals were rather cruelly ridiculed.

Peter had been standing around for some time when two men came up to him. One was a tall blonde fellow with an intelligent face and a tiny mustache under his nose. He introduced himself as Henry Klassen. The second, a dark-haired fellow of average height and well fed, said his name was Franz Rogalsky. They told him to take his luggage and follow them. They revealed to Peter that they would be his "parents." Klassen would he the "daddy" and Rogalsky the "mother". At the moment their remarks did not mean much to Peter, but it did not take him long to realize the significance of this relationship.

The new "parents" led their son into one of the several wings of the large building. It was the "Gypsy wing"' they said, and all the fellows living here were known as Gypsies. They pointed to another similar wing and said it was known as "the wing of the Moles" and a third as "the wing of the Jews." In each there were a number of rooms, large room numbers written on the doors. Because of this the men always referred to rooms always as a "number." One never said, for instance, "in our room," but rather "in our number."

Peter and his new "parents" entered a room with the number eleven on the door. It was a large, bright room with twelve single beds. Near each bed was a clothes closet and a small table. Four of the beds were not made. Wiens directed Peter to one of the empty beds and informed him that henceforth this would be his "farm."

On the bed lay a large empty sack and Peter was told to go and fill it with "colony downs," meaning with straw. At the strawstack Peter met several others, also filling their sacks. Some of them told him that when they returned to their rooms, their sacks would likely be weighed and quite possibly they might have to carry one or two straw blades back to the straw pile. It was their way of instructing newcomers not to use colony property recklessly. But Peter had no difficulties. His "parents" were reasonable, in fact they assisted him in making his to store his bed properly. They also showed him how clothes and his laundry and gave him a few valuable hints on how to conduct himself in this new environment. Peter congratulated himself on having found such sensible "parents."

In their room were eight old and four new recruits. Each of the newcomers had a pair of parents. "What for?' thought Peter. The answer was not slow in coming. Each man, for instance, had to keep his axe and his hoe sharpened. Good children, naturally, would not want the parents to do what they could do for them. Two newcomers would work together when it came to sharpening their tools. One would turn the wheel and the other hold the tool to the stone. Between the two they would have two axes and two hoes, but as good children they would also bring their parents tools and attend to them too. This gave six axes and six hoes to sharpen. As obliging children, they rendered other similar services to their beloved parents.

Peter soon discovered that the twelve men in his room came from various Mennonite settlements and belonged to different churches. Some came from well-to-do families others from poor ones. Some were well educated and others poorly. To live within such a group for three years had an educational value: itt broke the geographic isolation of the various settlements and to a great extent removed the traditional barriers between the various conferences. It also served as an equalizer between the social layers of the Mennonite brotherhood.

There was a library in the forestry camp. About two thirds of the books were in the German and the rest in the Russian language. A number of the men read extensively, some little and others nothing. Quite often lively discussions were carried on in the room. The older men did the talking; the newcomers were expected to listen and answer when asked. The men were saying that the Mennonites are very good with material things: they are practical and good organizers. But they have little appreciation for culture. They have often been hostile to culture. They have no folk songs and very few - if any - stories. Nothing like the Russian peasant who has a fruitful imagination and has çomposed many simple songs and created an endless number of folk stories. Mennonites have lived in Russia for more than a century without creating their own literature.

"Have we no individuals who could have produced such literature?" the men asked, "Even if we had, their talent could not have developed since few of our people were willing to support such creations, read them, discuss and evaluate them, and if worthy, buy them. Books can only be published if a fairly large group is willing to support such a venture financially. But as long as our people are not willing to do any ofthese things, no talent can develop in our midst."

"What do our people know of their own history?" they continued, "Nothing. Were any of our men told why they were rendering this and not the regular military service before entering the forestry service? Was it ever impressed upon them that this service was a privilege which put our people under ethical obligations? Never."

They discussed the catechetical instruction given in the congregations of the church Mennonites.** It was agreed that in some churches such instruction was very good while in others it did not amount to very much. In some places it was learning by memory answers whose meaning was poorly understood and lacked warmth and application to daily life. Because of this the Mennonite Brethren Church, when it came into existence in 1860, rejected all catechetical instruction. They did not want "a faith learned by heart." Was this a good solution? No, it was a serious mistake, a typically Mennonite reaction. Mennonites traditionally separated from those they disagreed with. It would have been wiser for the Mennonite Brethren church to retain the catechism instruction. The questions and answers could have led to constructive discussion and instruction.

Peter listened intently to the discussions in his room. He found them meaningful and instructive. They prodded his thinking and sharpened his desire to read and inform himself. He knew that not in all rooms did such an atmosphere prevail. He happened to be in a room with several well educated and intelligent men who set the tone for all of them. For this Peter was thankful.

Men who wished had a chance to enroll in various courses given by the better educated soldiers. They offered courses in

---

** Mennonite Conference Church

science, mathematics, Russian or German language, history or Bible. The superiors encouraged such studies and the men teaching had their workload somewhat reduced. A number of men took the opportunity, but there were also others who avoided all serious matters. They sat around in their free time, relating stale stories and telling old jokes and waiting for the end of their service. For them life began only when their service in the forestry unit was ended.

The men had to get up in the morning at the sound of the bell. For breakfast good white bread and boiling water was served. The men had their own coffee or tea and most had butter or jelly. But there were always some who could not afford any extras and who ate what was served. Very seldom did the wealthier men share with such a poor brother. Their upbringing was in part to blame. Consideration for their fellow men, for the weak, the poor or the deprived was hardly ever preached in our churches.

After breakfast the men marched into the forest to work. At noon they were served a good meal with meat. In winter it was mainly pork, but in summer mutton. The men noticed that during the time mutton was being served they were in better health than when they were eating pork. In spite of this they went back to pork for the winter, partly because the Mennonites of Russia were used to pork. At four o'clock bread and water was served, and in the evening a full meal but without meat. On Sundays and holidays a butter was served at breakfast and the coffee break in the afternoon. The meals were not fancy but they were nourishing. Most men were satistied but there were always some grumblers and complainers in any group. They had them at the forestry camp too.

There was full-time minister at the forestry camp. Every evening he conducted a brief service with the men and on Sundays and holidays a regular church service. Attendance at these services was obligatory. Once a week he conducted Bible study class for those men who wished to participate. A military officer, known as *Starshij****, was in charge of all the men. Three stripes on as his collar indicated his rank. He had three assistants known as "Gefreiter," a rank about equal to that of lance corporal in the regular army. These men did not a have to work themselves but were in charge of the command.

The position of the Starshij was not an easy one. He had to keep order among the 131 men. Most of the fellows were reasonable - many were fine men indeed - but there were also a few troublemakers. He had to know how to handle them. The Starshij had to be on fairly good terms with his men, who had no desire to overexert themselves, while the Forester, the government official in charge of the forestry canmp, wanted to get out of them as much as possible. The Starshij also had to keep his friendship, and reconcile the two extremes.

A special event was the visit of the Mennonite Forestry president, David Claassen. He spent a few days at the Forestry camp inspecting everything for which the Mennonite brotherhood had a responsibility. At a public meeting with the men he told them that the conferences and congregations were very much concerned about them. At every annual conference he had to report to the churches. He complimented the men. Years ago their conduct had not been all that the churches desired but during the last decade or so there had been a great improvement he told them.

He pointed out that they were enjoying a great privilege compared to other national groups, whose sons had to serve in

---

*** *Starshij* means literally "the oldest." The title was given to the man in charge of the Mennonite soldiers in the foresty service.

the regular army and nd be ready to lay down their life should war break out. But it was at great own cost to the brotherhood. He told them that 1,204 young Mennonites were in active service at a cost to the brotherhood of 347,492.73 rubles that year. Since the Mennonite brotherhood in 1913 had some 35,000 able-bodied workers and since a day's wage for a man during harvest time was about 1.20 rubles, the amount of money contributed by the brotherhood was a rather heavy burden. Nevertheless, it was a sacrifice the brotherhood was quite willing to make for the sake of their young brothers.

When he asked the men whether they had any complaints, a few such were voiced. The most common concerned the length of the working day, which varied from month to month. In January the men had to be outside eight hours per day, in February ten, in March ten and a half, in April twelve and during the following three months twelve and a half hours per day. In September the time sank to seven and a half hours. The men felt that in summer the hours of work were really too long and should be shortened. Claassen agreed their complaint was valid but he pointed out that in winter there was practically no work at all, since here in southern Russia work was mainly planting and cleaning forests, and very few trees were being cut. However, he would bring this matter to the attention of the proper authorities. The Forestry president David Ivanovitch Claassen established an excellent rapport with the Mennonite camps. He was 58 years old, a man of impressive personality, well educated, a minister of the Mennonite Brethren church. For some years he had served as Oberschulze of the Kuban Mennonite settlement where he owned a tract of land.

His sincere Christian faith and his kindness to the poor and the neglected made him popular among Mennonites and others.

For his out standing achievements in horticulture Claassen was honored by the Russian government. Peter considered himself privileged to be exposed to such a man.

CHAPTER THREE

YOUNG FOLKS

Peter Braun was the eldest son of a well-to-do Mennonite farm family in Margenau. After him came a younger brother and two sisters. He and his parents had never doubted that one day he would step into the shoes of his forebears and be a farmer as they too had been. After the completion of public school his parents had sent him to the *Zentralschule* at Gnadenfeld. The school had a three-year course and Peter had graduated with honors. He loved his studies and he loved books. He had skillful hands and could do with them almost anything that needed to be done on a farm.

In 1819 his great-grandfather had settled on the farm the Brauns lived on. Until then the regionhadbeen virgin soil. No plow had ever cut into this land. The wild Nogaies had pastured their skinny animals here and occasionally set up their tents in this region. In 1803 the Russian government, eager to have the land cultivated, granted 360,000 acres (144,000 hectares) to the Mennonite brotherhood and the next year the first Mennonite Villages were established along the Molotschna river. To every Mennonite family was given 180 acres of land.

Peter's great-grandfather had lived in the city of Danzig. On a Sunday in 1817, after the regular service, he was married to Maria Klassen and with his young bride and her parents he had come to southern Russia. When in 1819 the village of Margenau was settled, the young couple too had taken a homestead and settled here. They built their home and planted hundreds of trees. Since the house they built was large and well constructed, they must have brought money with them from Danzig. The great-grandfather broke some of his land, and when he eventually found his final resting place in the newly-established cemetery, Peter's grandfather had taken over the farm. He lived all his life here and continued the work begun by his father. He broke more land and added various buildings to the first house. Then he too was laid to rest and Peter's father continued the work. It was quite clear that one day Peter would continue to farm the fields three generations of Brauns had tended.

Often he wondered who his forebears might have been. What had they been doing in Danzig? Had his great-grandfather married Maria Klassen because he loved her or had it been a marriage of convenience, since no single man could pioneer at that time? He had found no answers anywhere to all his questions. It hardly ever happened that people talked about the far past; nor was anything along this line taught in school. In school he was made to study the history of the Jewish people in detail. He had to know the names of Jacob's twelve sons and remember the one daughter whose name was Dinah. All this was drilled into him and into other students, but about their own past, who they were, why they had come to southern Russia, of these things no one said even a word. In their homes all of them used the Low German language. In school they learned the High German and the Russian languages, but no one ever mentioned the Low German.

It was not dignified with even a single sentence. Peter marvelled at this and felt that it was totally wrong. But to the majority of the Mennonite people such thoughts apparently were alien.

In a certain respect the Brauns differed from other Mennonite farmers. Of the thirty or so farming families of Margenau, the Brauns were the only ones who had retained their farm since 1819. The average Mennonite sold his farm quite readily if this seemed to be to his advantage. He saw his acres as a source of income, as an object with which he was in no special way connected. The Braun family took a different attitude. They loved their home and their land. Here they had lived and worked for several generations. Here they had planted a garden. They saw their farm as a place that belonged to them, their home, their love. It was not for sale. Because of this there was never any doubt in Peter's mind that after his father's death he would continue to work this piece of land as his forebears had done.

But first he would have to render his service to his country. He did so quite willingly. He found his life here, the many contacts with other young men, quite stimulating. Among the three other recruits that shared his room there were two, John Wiens and Peter Klassen, who became his close friends.

John Wiens, too, was a farmer's son and his home was in the nearby settlement of Sagradowka. In fact, the villages of this settlement partly surrounded the Vladimirow forestry camp in which Peter was serving. The settlement consisted of sixteen villages with a total population of about forty-five hundred persons. Besides its German name each village also had a number. This was done because of their Russian neighbors. The Russians found the German names difficult, but they could very easily remember a number. The Mennonites themselves found the numbers simpler than the names and so they too usually referred to a village by its number. Most of the villages had traditional names, brought from villages in the area of Danzig when their people emigrated to the Ukraine.

John Wiens's home was in the village Number 4. On quite a few weekends he could go home. After a time he took his new friend Peter Braun with him and introduced him to his parents and brothers and sisters. Although the Sagradowka villages were situated several hundred miles from the Molotschna settlement, Peter found the buildings and life style practically identical to what he had at home. He felt at home in the Wiens' family right from the beginning.

Eventually Peter learned to know the young people of the village. There were three churches in the Sagradowka settlement and in summer meetings took place there; but in winter, when the roads were not too good, the villagers held their religious services in their own village public schools. This gave Peter an especially good opportunity to view the citizens of the village. Practically everybody attended the Sunday morning worship services. It was an unwritten law in a Mennonite vilage. On a Sunday morning the school building was usually nearly full. Occasionaly the village choir sang. The choir members sat up front facing the audience. This gave Peter an excellent opportunity to look at the young people, especially the girls, more closely. In the afternoon he and John would go to places where the young people, or at least a part of them, were meeting.

In practically all Mennonite villages association between the sexes was restricted. But old and young understood that it was necessary for young people to meet. In order to put a good face to the situation, the young people usually met in a home in which there were grownup sons and daughters. The boys of the village came to visit the son and the girls the daughter of the home. Most of the time the parents knew of such planned visits and so they went somewhat early to visit friends or relatives. They put their home at the disposal of the young people.

At first the boys likely met in the *Sommerstube* (summer room) and the girls in the *Eckstube* (corner room), but then they all gathered in the *Grosse Stube* (the great room). They talked, sang, made music and often played various games. Young couples who had a "understanding" but were not officially engaged, sat together. These young people behaved well. There was no objectionable conversation or suggestive jokes. The topics were not always very intellectual; they discussed the news of the village, asked Peter Braun questions about his village and the young people there, or talked about something they had read. Peter felt at home with them.

Although he was more than twenty years old, Peter had not had a steady girlfriend. At home he had occasionally been interested in one or another girl and had even gone out with them, but all this had been rather superficial. Nothing serious. His heart was not involved, but now he got to know a girl who appealed to him more than any other. Her name was Lena Martens and she was two years younger than he.

She was the daughter of a well-to-do farmer; a slim girl, she had dark brown hair and large brown eyes. Although Lena spoke easily, she weighed her words. Peter found they had much in common and he considered her an intelligent girl. Lena was neat in appearance. One evening Peter noticed that Lena tore a hole in her apron. A few days later when Peter again sat next to her, he couldn't help noticing that the damage had been very neatly repaired. He concluded that the girl must be a good housekeeper and she seemed to him more and more desirable.

The summer of 1914 had arrived. As often as possible, without becoming a burden to them, Peter would visit the Wiens' home in Number 4. On enchantingly beautiful summer evenings the young folk of the village gathered in some farmer's yard. They sang and played tag games Such as "Hasch, hasch" and others. Such games can be of interest only to unspoiled young people who are still strangers to passions, for whom a glance from beautiful eyes or a touch of the hand is quite sufficient. When one is young and at the threshhold of life, full of energy and the joy of life, the bewitchingly soft air, the silvery moon, and the mysterious darkness of the nearby garden make the present moment utterly beautiful and full of promise. A social evening with other young people under such conditions is a high point in life.

Peter was quite familiar with these social evenings. He had been part of similar evenings in his native Margenau. But never had they gotten such a hold of him as here in Sagradowka. Was it the contrast to the somewhat monotonous life in the forestry camp or was it the presence of Lena, who exerted a growing charm on him? He did not know. He only knew that he was happy and it seemed to him as if the future for him could not be otherwise but beautiful.

That July brought news that came as lightning from a clear sky. Russia and Germany were at war! The news rocked the Mennonite colonies. All wars are a misfortune, but a war with Germany was a tragedy for all those citizens of Russia whose mother tongue was German. *"What will such a war mean for us?"* was the question every thinking German living in Russia asked himself.

The young men of the country were immediately rushed into service, and only the young Mennonites for the time being were not called. At first it seemed the government did not know what to do with them, since according to the more than a century old agreement they did not have to serve in the actual army. But within about a month, a decision was reached: Mennonite men were to serve in Red Cross units, in offices, in forestry camps, in road building gangs and in factories. All young Mennonite men were ordered to appear before the authorities. The forestry camp at Vladimirow was ordered to send 50 of its men immediately, nearly half of its command, to Moscow to put them at the disposal of the Red Cross. Among those who had to go were also Peter Braun and his two friends. There was no time for him to say good-bye to his parents at home in Margenau, but he could have a few days to see his friends in Number 4. Most of all he wanted to see Lena.

At that time a young man could not simply go to the home of a girl to visit her without raising some serious questions. The separation of the sexes was too profound and to the stiff Mennonites such free relationships were alien. It never to occurred Peter to go directly to the Martens' home. But through John Wiens's cousin he sent a message to Lena asking her to meet him in the evening. Lena returned the word that at seven o'clock she would be waiting for him at the garden gate. At the agreed time Peter was at the gate. Side by side the couple walked slowly down the village street. Their hearts were full and heavy. At first they talked about the war: what could it possibly mean to all of them? And of Peter's service, of which no one at that time knew what form it might take. They talked about Peter's parents and of what Lena might be doing when most of the men of the village would have left to serve in the army.

Finally Peter said, "Lena, until now I've never been serious about any girl. But you have impressed me as no other girl. If I were free, I would ask you to marry me at the end of my current service. But I am not free. Tomorrow morning I'm leaving for the unknown. I have no idea what might happen to me. Possibly, they'll send me onto the battlefield to collect the wounded or into barracks to tend men suffering from contagious diseases. I may lay down my life in the near future or I may return home a cripple. I could also be taken prisoner by the enemy and not be heard from for years. It would not be right for me to ask a person dear to me to promise herself to my uncertain future. You must remain free, Lena. But I would like to ask you whether I may write to you and whether you will answer my letters. What do you say, Lena?"

"I shall be glad to hear from you, Peter," replied the girl, "and I shall write back. Please send me a picture of yourself as soon as you can. I'm glad that I learned to know you; my only regret is that my parents did not have this opportunity. I am sure that they would have liked you too. God be with you, Peter. Write me and come home safely again."

Peter took Lena's hands. For some time they looked at each other. Then Peter bent over and kissed her. It was a brief kiss, not the kiss of an experienced lover, but to both it meant more than long speeches. Peter left. Early next morning he and John Wiens were driven to the railway station. Peter Braun had reached a turning point in his life.

CHAPTER FOUR

IN A RED CROSS UNIT

At the station at Poltavka 50 young Mennonites took the train to Moscow. It was a direct train and took 43 hours to bring them to their destination. These are distances that for small European countries such as the Netherlands, Denmark or Switzerland would be simply incomprehensible. But in Russia there are much longer distances to travel. One has only to think of the Moscow-Vladivostok distance, which takes about eight days to cover.

For Peter the ride was enjoyable. He sat at the window and watched the passing landscape, the villages, the many stations crowded with all kinds of people. Peasant women offered fried chickens, cookies, fruit and milk for sale. Everywhere could be seen young men in uniform. The country was at war. Farther north they travelled through forests. To Peter, a son of the steppes, this was a new experience.

Then the name, Moscow, was called out. In school Peter had learned a great deal about this city, the heart of the mighty Russian empire. He knew Moscow from his readings, from poems and many stories. He knew about the many gold-covered church steeples, about the Kremlin, the Red Square, the Cathedral of St. Basil and of many other historical places. He had read and heard of them but now he was about to see them. That excited him.

At the station they were met by a sergeant who took immediate command. Their luggage was placed on wagons and they themselves had to form groups of fours and were marched to their barracks. This turned out to be a large three-story building containing quarters for the men, kitchens, dining halls and offices. Peter was given a bed and asked to put his things in a clothes closet. Then he had to register and was inspected and asked all kinds of questions. In the days that followed the newcomers had to drill for many hours each day. They learned to march and to salute officers; they were instructed about the various ranks of officers, the intention being to convert these farm boys into something resembling soldiers. Later they were told how to handle the wounded and the sick; how to load them onto a train or put them onto a bed, and what to do in an emergency. The men were informed that they would be placed on hospital trains which would bring the wounded from the battle fields to various cities in the hinterland. The need for such service was great and because of this they were pressured relentlessly to learn quickly what they had to know.

Russia at that time had three semi-military Red Cross organizations, two of which ran trains and the third maintained hospitals in many cities of the realm. Mennonites served in all three.

The mode of dealing with the men differed somewhat from organization to organization. In some, for instance, the men were supplied with government-issued clothing. They were taken into huge halls in which there were many stalls, each about twelve by twenty feet in size, and filled with one particular item of wear. For instance, in one stall were shoes, in another caps, in a third shirts, and so on. Each man was given a list of things he was to have and told to pick from the supplies in the room. This was not as simple as it might seem. The shoes, for instance, were individual; if a man found one shoe that fitted him, to find a companion among the thousands of shoes could be complicated.

Guards at the door inspected the men and their things so that no one would take more than what was coming to him. But human nature being what it is, stealing could not be prevented. Mennonite boys did not do it partly because each man knew that the rest of his group would take a dim view of stealing. But some of the students who volunteered to assist the soldiers in their search were not inhibited by such prejudices. They would appear one morning in ancient shoes and leave the same evening with new shoes on their feet. The next day they would show up in an old pair of pants and leave in the eveninng in a new pair. Such an exchange was practiced on many, possibly most, days. What they did not need themselves they knew could be sold.

In the branch of the Red Cross in which Peter was serving the men were not issued clothing but were given money from which to buy their uniforms. These were identical to those of the army except that their shoulder blades and their cockades indicated that they were Red Cross soldiers. Mennonite men practically always dressed well and made sure that their uniforms fitted them well. Peter, too, was converted into a fine young soldier. His made-to-measure military uniform was dressy and very popular at that time. As most others did, he had his photo taken and sent it to his parents, few of his friends and to Lena. He wondered whether he would please her in his new makeup.

The day came when the men received their assignments. About About 70 Red Cross trains, each a hospital on wheels and served by Mennonite men, were operating during the war. Peter Braun with thirty-six other men, was assigned to Train 189. His friend Peter Klassen was sent to Odessa where he was to serve on a Red Cross ship, and John Wiens, with whom he would have liked to remain together, was sent to the city of Rovno.

Train 189 was a hospital on wheels. It had many cars adapted to caring for the wounded and the ill. Then there were the cars in which the men and women serving on the train lived; one car served as an operating room, and another as a drug store and another as an office. The staff consisted of two medical doctors, several nurses, office workers, a few officials and the Red Cross soldiers.

Thirty-seven of the men on board were Mennonites, most of whom were soldier-nurses, officials or clerks. By now they knew that their organization trusted and appreciated them; though they also knew that in some places the hostility against all Germans was quite pronounced and that Mennonite men serving in such places were badly treated because of their nationality. There was no trace of such treatment in their organization, however; even the man in charge of all personnel, the Starshij, was a Mennonite named Neufeld. He was a public school teacher by profession, from the village of Friedensfeld, Molotschna, who was married and had two children.

To acquaint the medical corps with their duties the train undertook two short runs into the interior of the country. They loaded wounded in one city and transported them to another. Peter, along with the rest, was assigned to a single train car. There were twelve beds in his car. The wounded were brought in on litters and the litters fitted into frames. The men remained on them. If a wounded man had to be operated on he was carried on his litter into the operating room, a train car that had once carried passengers.

Eleven heavily wounded men were placed into one *teplushka* (railcar). The twelfth bed was reserved for the Red Cross soldier. It usually took about three nights to reach the destination. By this time the man looking after the wounded was tired-out and lice-ridden.

The badly wounded had to be looked after, fed and assisted; they had to be washed and turned over in their beds. All this had to be learned, and it could be learned too. As a group the Mennonites were conscientious and eager to do their very best. Their home training stood them in good stead: ther work ethic, their attitude to service and their well-taught Bible background, all combined to make them good - you might say, very good - in nursing the sick and wounded.

The lightly wounded were placed into special train cars with about thirty soldiers to a car and served by one Red Cross man.

Peter liked the work and sympathized deeply with the wounded men. Most of them were simple, ignorant peasants who suffered willingly for Mother Russia, although they had no property to defend and had been treated unkindly by their country. For these men Peter had an especialy warm heart. There were also the well-educated and obviously well-to-do among the sick and the wounded.

Peter was a diligent reader of the press. Quite often his reading left him unhappy. Not only did the papers report many outrageous stories about the brutality of the Germans, they also indulged in hate propaganda against the Russian citizens of German descent and this, Peter felt, included him too.

Occasionally the press reported on the Mennonite Red Cross soldiers and these reports were favourable. Thus he read in the *Russkija Vedomostji* of October 14, 1914 an article by the well-known Russian writer Count Alexej Nikolai Tolstoy, in which Tolstoy gave high praise to the Mennonites. Similar articles appeared from the pen of the Countess Alexandra L. Tolstoy and others who had been in contact with these soldiers. All gave credit to the Mennonite Red Cross workers for their self-sacrificing Christian service to the sick and the wounded.

After the two test runs in the interior, Train 189 was sent to cities like Warsaw and others close to the western front. From here the wounded were transported into the interior of Russia. On their way to the front the Red Cross workers were off duty and could take it easy, but on their return trip with the wounded they often had to be on their feet day and night and many nights in succession. After a number of such long rides the men of Train 189 had become quite proficient in their work.

CHAPTER FIVE

CAPTURED BY THE ENEMY

In January, 1915, Train 189 left Riga, where they had unloaded their wounded, and moved toward Warsaw. During the night of January 25 to 26 the train stood in the station at Vilna. While it was there, the alarm bell rang. The train had received an order to go immediately to the war front to the Wirballen train station where they were to pick up between 300-400 wounded men. In the early morning hours the train began its run over Kovno to its assignment. But aready in Kovno things began to look suspicious. On the road running alongside the railway, they saw endless columns of cavalry, infantry, artillery pieces and equipment moving in the opposite direction. The columns were in a great hurry and it was quite obvious that they were in retreat. The doctor in charge of the train tried repeatedly to contact his superiors to find out whether to proceed, but it was impossible to establish contact. The great haste of the retreating troops looked more and more like a rout.

The doctor was in a critical dilemma. His intellect told him not to proceed any further, but his orders said unequivocally, "Move ahead under all circumstances to pick up the last 300-400 wounded fighters."

Tne nurses were asked to prepare huge red cross flags which were attached to the sides and some to the tops of the cars. The train moved slowly forward. By now the stations on the line were only ruins. It was dark. In the West the sky was illuminated by great fires. The villages to their right and left were burning too. The retreating Russians were applying their ancient national tactic, the scorched earth policy. Nothing usable must fall into the hands of the enemy.

At about eight o'clock in the late afternoon of January 28 the train slowly inched into the Wirballen station. They found it crowded with hundreds of citizens. The train staff saw old panicking people, expectant women, mothers with crying children and men at their wit's end. The station was poorly illuminated. Wounded people crowded the floor of the waiting room, and they were now hurriedly loaded into the waiting train. Desperate and crying, citizens begged the Red Cross workers take them along and the men did not have the heart to to deny them. It was impossible to take everybody but they took as many as they could. Every inch of space on the train was occupied by fleeing men and women. Slowly the train began to pull out of the station. The men and women on the train began to congratulate themselves on the successful rescue of so many.

Then a mighty jolt! German orders were heard: "Out! Out!" It had happened. They had fallen into German hands.

Peter realized immediately that he now was a prisoner and his heart felt heavy. A feeling of helplessness swept over him; he knew that nothing could be done. He was a prisoner of war. Outside, voices were ordering everybody out of the train. Through the window he could see guns and bayonets. All who were able to walk left the train and only the badly wounded remained. When the Germans heard the Russian Red Cross workers speak German they were amazed!

"*Donnerwetter**," they exclaimed, "these fellows speak German!" They were informed that the Mennonite men had been Russian citizens for several generations although their mother tongue was German.

"Amazing!" the victorious Germans marvelled, and now they became quite friendly. The roughly shouted orders had been the result of the general excitement.

All those who could walk were ordered to raise their arms and walk into the station building. One Russian hoping to escape ran. The Germans ordered him to stop three times and when he did not obey they shot him dead.

The next morning the Red Cross personnel were ordered back to their train to tend the sick and the wounded the way they had been doing. The train remained standing for week. It rained ceaselessly. All around them was an indescribable mud and on top of it the excrement of the several hundred people in the train. It was a very difficult week. Slowly German doctors and officials brought order into the general mess.

The wounded were now transferred from the train into a building which was to serve as a temporary hospital. In fact there were two buildings: in one they placed the patients suffering from contagious diseases and in the other the soldiers who were simply

---

*Donnerwetter is an exclamatory phrase that literally translates as 'thunder weather.'

injured. Peter and twelve other Mennonites were assigned to the contagious hut. Most of the patients a were sick of typhoid fever, a very contagious illness. Yet during the two months they were here not one of the Mennonite boys became ill. They were well fed the whole time. The Germans had captured immense Russian supplies and could well afford to feed their prisoners well.

After two months the men were sent into a regular prisoner of war camp. Here they were fed poorly and life was boring. The men found it hard to live together with coarse people, to be totally idle and have no prospect of a change. Such conditions made them listless and indifferent. In May they were transferred to a camp for non-military war prisoners. Most of the inmates were Polish peasants and Jews. They had a lifestyle of their own. In their pockets they carried herrings covered with salt crust inside and out, which had been given to them. To live with such people, to endure the lice, the stench of poor tobacco, the coarse conversation, was for them pure torture. By summer an epidemic broke out in the camp of which fifteen to twenty people died daily. Among these was Gerhard Koop, the youngest of the Red Cross men, who had joined the unit as a volunteer and whose parents lived in the Sagradowka settlement. Food was so scarce that some of the inmates cried from hunger. Contact with their loved ones was very difficult. The first very brief letter received from home by any of them arrived five months after their capture.

Peter Braun was among those who tried not to give way to despair or indifference. He was physically well, tried to keep clean as far as this could be done, exercised daily and tried not to stunt his intellect. He recited poems songs he had once learned by heart, and busied himself with mathematical problems. Anything to keep his mind from deteriorating. It difficult but not impossible to obtain serious books to increase his knowledge. Among the prisoners were also several intelligent and well-informed men. Peter sought their company and profited from their association. From time to time prisoners were allowed to leave the camp to work in a factory or on a farm, though only the prisoners who wanted such work were handed over to some employer.

CHAPTER SIX

PRISONER IN GERMANY

One day a man and his wife came into their camp looking for a farm hand. Among the prisoners the tall Peter Braun stood out. The couple noticed him and told the overseer that he would be their man. When they found out that he spoke perfect German they determined to have him and no one else.

"Do you want to go with these folks?" the camp afficer asked Peter. "You'll have to work on their farm, give satistfactory service and conduct yourself so they'll have no just cause to complain. You are to be treated well, fed well but you'l not be paid for your work. Any time you are dissatisfied you may return to the camp."

Peter had been observing the couple carefully and concluded that they were good people. Since life in camp was hard to bear, he decided to go with them. And so Peter Braun left the prisoner of war camp to become a farmhand for the Mueller family.

The Muellers had a fair sized farm not far from the Dutch border. They were about 30 years old. The man was tall and slender and made a good impression, although he was not very well. Because of his poor health he had to watch himself constantly. His wife was a healthy and pleasant woman. They were very glad to have been given a helper and especially since this man spoke German perfectly and was a farmer's son, familiar with farm labour. It could not have been better, they said.

Peter was given his own clean room. The food was good, although different from what he was used to at home. Peter congratulated himself on having escaped the deadly monotony of the prisoner's camp and its filth and hopelessness. Though the work was somewhat different from what he had known at home, Peter had no difficulty in adjusting to it. He had grown up thinking that German farmers were much more progressive than were the Mennonite farmers in Russia. But he found this not to be the case. True, they were far ahead of the Russian peasants in their farming, but not of the Mennonites of Russia. In many ways these were more efficient. Weather conditions too were less favourable than they were in the Ukraine.

The Muellers were friendly and the work they demanded of Peter was not unreasonable. They were Catholics and appeared to be loyal adherents of their church. The couple was childless. Peter should have been fully content. In a way he was happy, but away from his comrades he had more time to think of his loved ones at home. The sunny Ukraine became very attractive to him. He had no contact with anyone except his employers. No one was willing to associate with a "Russian" and a prisoner at that. Neither did his employers associate much with their neighbors. The visiting which was customary in the Molotschna seemed unknown here and social customs were quite different. Farmers met their neighbors occasionally on the boundaries of their property, conversed for a while and then parted again. That was about all the visiting they did. Young people or community met in restaurants where they played and danced. Peter, of course, was not invited. For him, a Russian war prisoner, all such social life was unthinkable. But even if he had been asked to join in, he would not have cared to do so. His outlook on life was totally at odds with what was going on around him. He had no desire to be involved in any of the so-called pleasures of the local young people. He did a good deal reading; and in his free time he went for lengthy walks, talked with his employers or waited for the time when he could return to his homeland.

One day the Catholic priest came to visit the Muellers. Peter was presented to of him. The priest was a man about forty years, tall, and with an intelligent but cold face. He talked readily with Peter. He was surprised to learn that there were about two million Germans living in Russia and that large areas were populated almost exclusively by them. He listened with interest to Peter's description of the life of the Russian people and conditions in that country. For Peter the meeting was a pleasure. Here was an intelligent man who was interested in him and his homeland and who was able to understand and appreciate what Peter was saying.

From then on the priest showed up quite frequently in the home of the Muellers. Whenever he came Herr Mueller ordered Peter to entertain the priest. Never mind the work, it can wait, he would say. The priest knew how to pose questions and Peter willingly answered them. The priest also showed interest in Peter personally and soon he knew much about Peter, including that he was single and who his parents were and what they were doing.

One day he surprised Peter with a question. "How do you like Frau Mueller?" the priest wanted to know. "Quite well," replied Peter. He had no cause for complaints. "No, no," said the priest, "how do you like her as a woman?" Did she appeal to him? Peter didn't know what to say, but finally he answered that he hadn't given it a thought. Yes, he added after a while, she was an attractive woman.

Would you be willing to sleep with her?" the priest asked. Peter was dumbfounded. He thought he hadn't understood correctly. "Yes," the priest repeated, "I want to know if you would be willing to sleep with Frau Mueller." The priest explained the situation. These people were Catholics and well-to-do, but they were childless. When they died the farm and all their property would go to Protestant relatives. They should have children of their own, but Mueller was not able to father a child. Frau Mueller's greatest wish was to have a child, and if she did, their inheritance problem would be solved. In order that the farm could remain in Catholic hands it was necessary for her to have a child.

Peter was stunned. He had never known a woman intimately, he confessed, and here they were dealing with married woman living with her husband. ""How do you view that situation?" Peter asked.

"Well," replied the spiritual father, "that can all be solved. Just now, all we need to know is whether you are willing to play the part we've chosen for you."

"No," replied Peter. "I couldn't do it." His conscience would never permit him. In his view, the priest was inviting him to commit adultery and a sin. The priest did not press the matter any further. He said he had just wanted to know how Peter felt about the matter.

From then on Peter looked at Frau Mueller with different eyes. Had the priest spoken for her and with her knowledge? Did Herr Mueller know about the discussion and was he agreeable to the deed? Not once with even a single glance or word did Frau Mueller show that she had designs on him. Her conduct remained as it had been, discrete and above reproach. Peter concluded that for the time being the whole plan must have existed only in the mind of the priest. Had he consented to it, the priest would have tried to win the woman alone or possibly her husband as well for the scheme. But he never touched on this subject again. He acted as if he had said nothing out of the ordinary, but from then on Peter saw him with different eyes. This priest was utterly unscrupulous, and willing to do practically anything for his church.

CHAPTER SEVEN

JOHN WIENS' STORY

John Wiens, Peter's friend, and a number of other men were sent to the city of Rovno and placed in the three local military hospitals. John happened to be the only Mennonite in one of them. For some time he worked as orderly and then he was assigned to a night shift. It was customary in these hospitals to employ untrained peasant girls, in the city to earn a living, as assistants to the nurses. Such girls had to tend to the normal needs of the wounded and sick, make their beds and do other kinds of work that did not require special training. Each large hospital room had a Red Cross soldier assigned to it. He had to do the work that was too heavy or unsuitable for a woman to do. These soldiers were often Mennonites.

John Wiens was given a night shift and assigned to serve some forty patients. A girl named Tanja was in charge of the room and John had to assist her. In case of an emergency, they rang for a nurse or even a doctor. Some nights John and Tanja were busy but quite often they had little to do. The men slept more or less peacefully, and the two young people sat in the poorly lit room ready to serve when they were needed.

Tanja was nineteen years old and a good-looking, pleasant girl. At first the two, the young Mennonite and this girl, were shy with each other. But as they sat together without interruption night after night, not allowed to sleep, it was unavoidable that they became friendly with each other. Tanja told about her family, the village she came from, the life in her village and about her friends and her childhood. John related about his life and his background. They were young, thrown together by circumstances and alone. Tanja was good-looking and attractive. Neither of them planned it, but one night the inevitable happened - they lost their innocence. Both were inexperienced and for both it was the first time.

The relationship between them continued and deepened. Tanja loved her man as passionately as only a Slavic woman can. John liked the girl very much; he not only appreciated her more and more, but he also came to respect her. She was a good girl, sincere and pure. But John was far too sober a Mennonite not to know that there could be no union for life. Their backgrounds were too different. He could never bring this girl home. His family and the villagers would never accept her. And to stay in the city and to break permanently with his family and the life he was familiar with he could not do.

John had been brought up in a Christian family and Christian principles had been drilled into him. He knew that what he was doing was contrary to all that he had been taught. He had not sought this attachment and Tanja had not wished it, but both had been put into a situation which had overwhelmed them. Their loneliness in the big city and their natural human instincts had trapped them. John was often deeply disturbed by his inner turmoil.

There was another element. At home John had a steady girlfriend with whom he had an understanding that they would marry. Until now he had been corresponding with Anna. After the affair between him and Tanja he stopped writing to the girl. What could he say? Anna soon began inquiring why he had stopped writing: had she somehow offended him? Was there someone else? John did not reply. He tried not to think of the future.

Then one day he developed a pain in his chest. He went to see a doctor, who examined him closely and then told him that his heart was in poor shape. It was not really serious but enough for him to be careful, he was told. John was in no shape to do strenuous work and he would send him before a medical commission, the doctor said. He assured John that he would be dismissed from military service. When John appeared before the commission he was indeed released from all military obligations and told he was a free man again.

How often had he dreamed of being allowed to return to his friends and his parents. But as things had turned out, there was no joy in his heart. He was a marked man, a man with a twice-wounded heart. John had been told that despite of this weakness, he could live to a good age provided he was careful. Still John felt depressed because of his illness.

Weighing even more heavily was the affair with Tanja. How was it to be resolved? He had to say good-bye to her, and there was no hope that he would ever see her again. Had he wronged this good girl?

"Tanja,'" he said, "I am going home, and I will never be able to see you again. This is a parting for life. I hadn't meant to harm you and still I did it. I hadn't planned to seduce you. I like you very much; I will never be able to forget you. Do you hate me, Tanja?"

"Never, Johnny, I will never hate you. I love you with all my heart and I'll remember you as long as I live. You didn't deceive me. What happened has happened. Neither of us planned it and neither of us sought it, but we couldn't resist our fate. Our fate decreed that we should meet, and I do not regret it. If you say there is no future for us, and we must part forever, then so be it. I am happy that I came to know you. I will remember you always. My darling, think of me too once in a while."

John felt that his heart would break. He was deeply unhappy. The train brought him home. His parents were surprised. They were glad to have their son back again, but they were unsure whether the price was too high. However, after examining John their family doctor assured them the young man could live to a ripe age. Provided he was careful, he could live a normal life.

Yet John was terribly unhappy. He hardly left the house on his free days. He avoided his former friends and never went near Anna's place. Intuitively Anna understood that John was going through a crisis and that the best she could do was to give him time to come to terms with himself. One day John's father spoke to him. "Son, you are different from what you used to be. It is plain that something is bothering you and that you are deeply unhappy. Would you like to talk to me about it? Perhaps I could help, and putting your problem into words might help you too. After all, we are father and son."

John was quiet for a while. "It is true, Father, I am not happy," he said finally. "The service, my illness and all that I've experienced has upset my life. But I can't talk about it - not yet. I must find my own way out of my difficulties."

"As you wish, son," said Mr. Wiens. "But there is something I would like to mention. Before you went into the service, you used to keep company with Anna, but since your return you've not even been over to see her. Is there something wrong between you, John?"

"That is part of my problem, Father. I don't know what to do. I need more time."

"I understand you, but don't hurt Anna; she is a good girl and your mother and I would welcome her into our family if you should ever bring her home."

John made no reply. He continued to say nothing about his troubles until one evening he told his father he was going to see Anna. When he unexpectedly appeared before her, Anna paled a little and then immediately regained her composure.

"Good evening, John," she said. "I am pleased to see you." She spoke with restraint. She neither displayed great joy at seeing him nor did she play the part of the offended party. She acted as though they had just parted and nothing of significance had even passed between them.

"Anna," John began, "I am very miserable. I must speak to someone but I cannot think of anyone except you to speak to. Will you hear me? I know I don't deserve your kindness."

"I am glad you've come, John," she replied, "Yes, I am willing to listen to you, if you feel you want to share with me what is on your mind."

John poured out all that had happened during the last year. The story of Tanja and all that went with it, why he had stopped writing, and the inner turmoil he was going through. Anna listened quietly. Only now and then when she would she interject with a brief question when she couldn't understand. Not once did she reproach him.

When he had told all, John concluded, "I never meant to deal dishonestly with you or with Tanja, but I was weak, and I let the circumstances carry me away. I have hurt others and I've hurt myself too. I know what I did was wrong. Now that I have come home with poorer health, I have no claim on you, but I felt I owed you an explanation. I know that I was attracted to that other girl. And she is a good girl too, but I never loved anyone but you, Anna. No one understands me as you do and to no one can I talk as I do to you. I have lost you but at least I wanted you to know what happened and how I feel."

"What do you plan to do now?" asked Anna in a low voice.

"I don't know. I have no plans," John replied, "Life seems like a desert before me, without a road or water or shade. I shall manage, I hope."

"Wouldn't it be easier if we joined hands and walked this road together?" asked Anna, looking straight at John.

"Would you really consider that, Anna?" he asked, eagerly.

"I would not only consider it, I would be very happy to do it," said Anna, "I love you John, and understanding and forgiving is part of love. Let me be your companion for life, my darling."

John took Anna's hands and a few months later John Wiens and Anna Wiebe were married.

CHAPTER EIGHT

A SAILOR'S DEATH

Peter Klassen, John Wiens's friend, and a dozen other Mennonites were ordered to report to the marine authorities in Odessa. There they learned that two ships had been made ready in the Odessa harbour to serve as Red Cross hospital ships. One, the *Portugal*, had 1,800 beds for sick and wounded patients, and a staff of 262, 13 of whom were Mennonites. Peter Klassen was one of the 13.

The war against the Turks was being fought in an isolated region from which the casualties had to be evacuated by sea. The Red Cross ships, the *Portugal* and her sister ship the *Equator* transported them from the Turkish side of the Black sea to Batum. Each had made several runs. There were German U-boats in the sea who had sunk a great number of Russian ships. So far they had not bothered the Red Cross ships. But in March, 1916 the German commander of a U-boat contacted the captain of the *Portugal*. This ship had a radio antenna and the German ordered that the antenna removed. Radio contact, he said, could be used to inform the Russian authorities of the whereabouts of the German U-boats. A neutral ship such as the *Portugal* should not be doing this. The antenna had to go. But the

Russian captain just laughed and left the antenna in its place. He felt that the Germans would not dare to attack a Red Cross ship.

On March 17 the *Portugal* rode at anchor in front of Trabzon. About two thousand sick or wounded lay on the shore waiting to be evacuated. Small boats were to bring the men on board. Just then the periscope of a U-boat became visible. The boatman rushed to the bell to sound a warning, but the captain, his revolver drawn, stopped him. It was a Russian U-boat, he claimed, there was no danger. Suddenly the U-boat shot a torpedo parallel to the ship. Now the people on board realized the danger they were in and rushed for the safety belts. The U-boat meanwhile changed its position and with a second torpedo hit the 490 foot long ship in the middle. A terrible explosion burst the ship into two parts.

Chaos resulted. People ran from one end to the other. Some jumped into the cold waters, others did not dare to and went down with the ship. A hundred and five men lost their lives, among them two Mennonites, Peter Klassen and Peter Koehn.

CHAPTER NINE

JAKOB BRAUN MARRIES

Turkey, the traditional enemy of the Russians, was an ally of Germany. Nine and a half Russian infantry and seven cavalry divisions faced the old enemy. This was known as the Caucasian front. In February, 1916 the Russians took the Turkish fortress of Erzurum by assault and that spring Trabzon fell into Russian hands. The military hospitals naturally followed the invading armies and Red Cross trains carried the sick and wounded back into Russian cities, though mainly to Batum. Jakob Braun, Peter's brother, served in one of these trains.

Jakob, a tall young man, personable and fluent in speech, had graduated from the Gnadenfeid Zentralschule. He was to assigned serve in his train's office as secretary and bookkeeper. His assignment continued for some time during which he was given several leaves to visit his home. In the line of duty he came repeatedly to Tbilisi where the headquarters of the Red Cross was located. He also learned to know a number of the officials there and they in turn had come to appreciate the efficient bookkeeper.

In spring of 1916 one of Jakob's supervisors, the medical doctor in charge of the train, said to him, "Braun, I have an order for you to transfer to our headquarters in Tbilisi. The men there have taken a liking to you. They have a position for you. I hate to part with you - you have given excellent service. However, we are in the army and in the army. It is not customary to ask for the likes and dislikes of the individual. I have no choice but to comply. Tomorrow I shall appoint someone to take your place. You have six days to introduce the new man to his work and hand over your duties to him. Then you must leave. You have to report to your new place of service on May 15th at 9AM. Good luck, Braun. For you this is a promotion."

To Jakob the shift was not entirely unexpected. The possibility had been hinted at during his last visit to Tbilisi. But he did not know whether to rejoice or be disappointed. Now he was with fellow Mennonites, which to most of the men, including Jakob Braun, was valuable, yet the life on wheels in enemy country had its disadvantages too. Likely he would be the only Mennonite in his particular office in Tbilisi, though he knew that several other Mennonite men were serving in that city. Tbilisi is the Georgian term for "hot" and the city is so called because of the many warm sulphur baths nearby. It is picturesquely situated and compared to what the war front could offer in amenities, seemed like the epitome of comfort.

At the right time Braun reported to his new place of service. He was received kindly and appointed to the position of manager of an office section. This position raised him to the rank of a lieutenant, administration section. In the Russian Imperial Army there were three main branches of service: the active army, the medical corps and the administrative sections. Men serving in any one of the branches had identical uniforms, only the colours of the shoulder blades indicated the particular section.

As on officer, Jakob Braun was entitled to live in a private home. He found himself a suitable room not too far from his office. For the first few months he had very little free time. He had to acquaint himself with his new duties and with what had been going on in the past in the section for which he was responsible. The work was not too difficult, but for several months every waking hour belonged to his work. Then things became easier, and he had some free time on his hands. The city and the beautiful environment interested him and he spent many an hour inspecting its sights.

Tbilisi is an ancient city, and has been controlled by various national groups - Byzantines, Persians, Turks, Russians, and others. Its appearance tells the story of its past: here one sees well-built Russian quarters with wide streets and next to it Oriental sections with narrow streets and crowded bazaars. Here stand ancient cathedrals and modern theatres side by side. Jakob enjoyed wandering through the streets and visiting outstanding landmarks.

Before long, however, Jakob began to crave the fellowship of other people. He got in touch with some other Mennonites serving in the city and he also came to know socially some of his co-workers. In one of their homes one evening he made the acquaintance of a young graduate nurse named Nina. She was slim, with regular features, black eyes and hair and a melodious voice. Jakob liked her and something told him that this girl would become important to him.

Jakob Braun and Nina met quite often after their first meeting. Before long she invited him to her home and introduced him to her family. The Shapovalovs, Nina's parents, lived on a quiet and pleasant street and in a neat and attractive house. They and Nina's two younger sisters were friendly and easy to talk to. They received the young man their daughter had brought home like an old friend.

There was nothing stiff and artificial about them. In the course of the evening they asked a few questions about his background and his parents but not in an inquisitive way. Jakob felt quite relaxed with the family.

Jakob Braun visited the Shapovalov home quite frequently after that. He came to them quite well and they in turn introduced him to their friends. In many ways he found these people different from the folks in Margenau. They conversed on practically any topic under the sun; they sang; they recited poems; they discussed literature and political news. Many of these topics he had never heard discussed by anyone. Yes, the fathers in Margenau talked politics, but literature? Never. It simply did not exist for them. Singing? Yes, the young people sang a great deal and many good songs. German and Russian, but in mixed gatherings, where older and young folks met he had never heard singing. In the Mennonite villages there was a rigid division of old and young. These Russians were quite different: among them old and young mixed much more readily.

The Shapovalovs were members of the Greek-Orthodox church. Nina invited Jakob to accompany her to church and this too was for him a new experience. Everything about the church was very different from what he had known until now. The structure itself followed characteristic Orthodox architecture and was richly decorated with icons and frescos. To Jakob the icons seemed to be stiff, archaic and expressionless. There were no seats in the church and all visitors stood during the service. Despite the absence of musical instruments, a well trained choir sang a number of songs. During the service the priest wore an elaborate gown. The incense that he burned filled the building with a pleasant odor. He used the old Slavonic language which was no longer under stood by the common people. Hundreds of candles were burning. Up front in this church were two coffins of individuals who had died centuries ago and were declared to be saints. Visitors bought candles, lighted them and set them in front of one or the other of these coffins, prayed before the coffins and kissed them. To Jakob it all seemed very strange; he found it fascinating since it was new to him but inwardly the experience left him totally cold. Not so to Nina. She crossed herself many times, bought a candle and set it up in front of an icon of the mother of God. She prayed standing in front of this icon for some time and it was obvious that she was moved. Jakob could not follow what she was doing and did not share her feelings.

The day came when Jakob realized that he was deeply in love with Nina. At first the realization frightened him. Nina was not a girl to be trifled with and he for that matter was not a man who wanted to treat a girl lightly. If there was to be anything more than friendship between them it would have to be marriage. But they were from two different worlds. In religion alone they differed greatly. Jakob had received a thorough religious training. His parents had taught him, and in the village school as well as in the Zentralschule he had been given a lesson in Bible or church history every day. He was thoroughly imbued with Protestant-Mennonite concepts, and these differed greatly from those of the Orthodox church. As expected of him Jakob had taken the catechetical instruction in his parents church and was baptised. He had not submitted to baptism lightly. He had been convinced that his church was teaching the way to salvation clearly and biblically. He had prayed to God, had confessed all his known sins and had seriously resolved to be guided in life by the precepts of God. Jakob had not experienced a conversion similar to Paul's. His development could be compared to the experience of Lydia of whom it was said, "The Lord opened her heart to give heed to what was said." Jakob too had said yes to the still soft voice in his heart.

Now he had been away from home for more than two years and very seldom had fellowship with believers. Although he had a Bible with him, given to him by his parents, he hardly ever read in it. He had stopped praying formally long ago, though in his heart he still spoke to God and asked for guidance and thanked him on special occasions. Jakob knew that spiritually he was not what he should be and once had meant to be, but from the things which were obviously wrong and coarse, he definitely dissociated himself from.

Nina was a fine girl. She believed in God and prayed to him, and as she was taught, prayed also to the saints, asking for their intercession. Their concept as to what right and what was wrong likely would be the same but their theological views differed greatly. How that work out in married life?

If he married Nina, Jakob knew he could not bring her to his village. She would remain a stranger; she would not feel at home and the Mennonite people would make no effort to make her feel at home. To marry Nina would mean he would have to remain in Tbilisi, join her people and break with his own. Yet he could not readily consent to this either and he did not have the will power to do the only thing that could have helped him - break with the girl and not see her any more. The result was that events took their natural course and one evening, sitting in the parlor of the Shapovalovs, he said to Nina: "There is something I wanted to say to you for some time, and I am sure that you knew that I would say it. I cannot postpone it any longer. I love you, Nina: I love you with all my heart and I am asking you to marry me. Tell me you will, darling."

To Jakob's consternation Nina began to cry uncontrollably. He was shaken. "What is the matter, Nina? Have I offended you? Why are you crying?"

Nina could not answer. After a time, when she had calmed down, she said, "Forgive me, Jascha. When a girl is told by the man she loves that he loves her too, she should rejoice. I would like to, but I can't. I love you, Jascha; I love you with all my heart. But when you ask me whether I want to become your wife, I must answer no. That's why I'm crying. In fact, now that we have confessed to each other how we feel, we must part and never see each other again."

"But why? why? I don't understand!" exclaimed the young man. "Can't you see?" came Nina's quick reply, "You are a German and I am a Russian, and though that need not be a hindrance, it does create problems. But with you a Protestant and I as an Orthodox believer, that makes it more challenging. I cannot give up my faith and you will not give up yours. And where would we live? You would want to take me to your Mennonite village, where people speak a language I don't understand and live a life which is unknown to me. I could not be happy there. It would poison our relationship, Jascha. I love you and to me you are all I could desire in a man, but it would be disastrous for us to man. We would only make each other miserable. No matter what our hearts desire, we have no common future; we must part tonight forever."

"But we cannot do that, Nina," Jakob pleaded, "I have thought about this matter for a long time and I agree that I cannot ask you to live in our villages. I am willing to stay here with your people and become one of you. One day I hope we shall be able to visit my parents. I want you to meet them - I do not wish to break with them - but we shall live with your parents here or in any other city we shall agree on. As far as your church is concerned, it is true that

I can never become a member of it, but you can remain one. I won't put any obstacles in your way. I know it would be better if both of us were members of the same congregation and could share our spiritual life in full. And to some extent we can, since both of us believe in God and his son Jesus Christ and both of us expect to be saved by the grace of God. We may differ in how we approach this common God, but that need not be too great an obstacle. There is one possible solution that could bring us together into one church. Here in your city is a small Russian Baptist congregation. I would feel at home there and if you could too, we would be completely united, but I shall never insist that you take this step. You will be free to follow your conscience. What do you say, Nina?"

"If you are willing to make these sacrifices, Jascha," came the soft response, "I think we have a chance. I am only too glad to take it. I love you with all my slavic soul, my hero, and I would be happy to become your wife as soon as you wish."

That same evening the two young people spoke to Nina's parents and asked for their consent to their marriage. The parents, of course, had been aware of how the young people felt to each other and they had the same concerns as those Nina had voiced. They liked and respected Jakob as a man and happily welcomed him into the family. The wedding, it was agreed, would take place in the family's church and be performed according to the Orthodox rite.

* * *

Some time later the Jakob Brauns in Margenau received a letter from their son Jakob. Since no mail was operating at the time the letter had been passed from hand to hand by returning soldiers, as was quite common at that time. They read it eagerly:

Dear Father and my dear Mother:

For many months I have not heard from you, but I hope that you are well. I also hope this letter comes into your hands. I am afraid that what I have to say may hurt you very much. You are the last people in the world I would like to hurt, but I do not know how I could have avoided this.

Since May 5, 1918, I am a married man. I am married to a Russian girl by the name of Nina Shapovalov. She is a good and beautiful woman and I love her very much. Her parents and her two sisters also live here in Tbilisi. Nina is an educated woman, by profession a graduate nurse, and works here in the local hospital. I am still at my former job. We do not own many worldly goods but we earn our living, have rented a few rooms and are very happy.

I know how you feel about such marriages, but I hope that you will try to understand us. The Bible says that man will leave father and mother and cling to his wife.

That seems to be the fate of us men. If I had remained in our village I would not have been put into a situation where my choice and your wishes would have conflicted. I did not leave home because I wanted to; I was forced to do so. I met Nina and fell in love with her very much against my wish. I couldn't help it and neither could she. Please accept us as your children and try to love us both. I never meant to disappoint you, even if I did.

You will understand that I cannot bring my Russian wife into our settlement. What would be her future there? She would be a stranger and isolated and miserable. Happiness would be impossible. That is why I promised Nina that I would remain here with her folks. We would love to visit you sometime if you will have us and political conditions will permit. I do not doubt that you will come to love my darling once you have come to know her. She is lovable and good.

As far as our church ties are concerned, Nina is a member of the Orthodox church and to her this church is dear. I was brought up differently, believe differently and could never join her church, but I have promised not to put any obstacles in Nina's way. And we want to try to find common ground in our spiritual life also.

Dear parents, I could not help what I have done. I love my young wife with all my heart. If you can, please accept Nina as your daughter-in-law. She wants to love you too. She is including a letter to you. We would be overjoyed to have you tell us that you accept us both as your children. I love you, my dear parents and my dear brothers and sisters. God be with you all.

Your son and brother,

Jakob.

Nina had written a friendly letter and enclosed it with her husband's writing.

When Kathe had read both letters to her parents, they sat numbly for a number of minutes and said nothing. Their entire upbringing and the practice within the colonies made the marriage of a Mennonite to a Russian, no matter how good a person, seem like a violation of nature and God's law. The Mennonite church had come into existence in 1525, and at best had always only been tolerated by the countries they lived in. The laws of some of these countries had forbidden an outsider to join a Mennonite church. Marriage of a Mennonite to an outsider meant that they had to leave the Mennonite church and break with their family. What at first was imposed upon the Mennonite people in the course of time became the norm. They became ingrown and ethnocentric, Now they had lived in Russia for a century, surrounded by ignorant peasants, and this had strengthened their ethnic feelings very much. The Russian law, up to the revolution, stipulated that when Mennonite married a Russian he became by that act a member of the Orthodox faith. For a Mennonite to a marry Russian therefore meant to give up his language, his faith and his nonresistant position. No wonder that such step came to be looked upon as nearly unthinkable.

When a member of a Jewish family married a Christian, the family would invite friends and relatives to asymbolic funeral. From then on the one that had left the Jewish community was dead as far as they were concerned. Neither parents nor family members nor anyone else had any contact with that person from that day on.

The Mennonites never went that far. Before 1917 such marriages were very rare indeed, but when they occurred family bonds were not completely broken. Visits between such a mixed family and their Mennonite relatives still continued.

The Brauns made no immediate decision. They had to have time. It was a terrible blow to the parents, but they had no intention of being hasty with an answer. Time would find a solution to this problem as it finds for practically all situations in life.

CHAPTER TEN

PETER'S BID FOR FREEDOM

Peter Braun's disillusionment with the priest strengthened his longing for his homeland and his family. Molotschna was his real homeland. The Mennonites had lived there a little over a century, but in that time they had developed a love and an attachment to their new home that they had never felt for their former home in the Danzig area, though they had lived there much longer. Slowly he developed a plan. He thought of it so often that he finally became a prisoner of it: he would try to get home. He knew that the Dutch border only about fifty miles away. It should be possible for him to get across this all-important line. Once in Holland would be safe and able to find help, since there were Russian diplomats there. These people would gladly help him, he thought. The more he thought of it the plausible the plan seemed to become. He finally decided that he would flee. All that remained was to plan every step in detail.

Slowly and piecemeal to avoid suspicion, he gathered information about the border. Was it guarded? Could ordinary citizens cross from one country to another? From a map he studied the from way to the frontier and committed it to memory. He obtained old clothing belonging to Herr Mueller that would give him the appearance or a local citizen. He had to make himself appear much older than he was. All young Germans these days in wore the Kaiser's uniform and a healthy young man in civilian clothes would arouse suspicion. He would have to take some food with him because it would be too risky for him to enter a public building. He would have to travel nights only - and they had to be dark nights at that. When he was ready and the time seemed to be right, Peter wrote a note to the Muellers, thanking them for all their kindness to him. He had no complaints against them, he assured them, but he had an unconquerable longing for his homeland and his loved ones. He simply had to try to get home. He left the letter in a place where he hoped that it would be found, but not immediately; he had to give himself a little time. The Muellers would have to report his disappearance as soon as they became aware of it. He figured that he might have a head start of ten to twelve hours; then the search for him would be on. Peter was aware that he was embarking on a dangerous mission, but he had played with the thought of getting home so often and for so long now that it seemed impossible to give up the plan.

One evening, after dark, when the Muellers believed him to be in bed, Peter left. He made good progress, walking all night and into the morning as long as he dared. Then he hid himself in an old granary standing some distance from the road. Here he spent most of the day sleeping. As soon as it was dark he was on his way again. He knew that by now the alarm would have been given and that men would be looking or him. Therefore, he had to be extra cautious. He avoided the highway and was careful with his food supply. He had enough of it he felt, but he had nothing to drink and he did not dare to enter a farmyard in search of water. Even if the farmer did not notice him, the dogs certainly would. All they needed to do was to raise an alarm and he was done for. It was better, therefore, to suffer thirst, Peter concluded.

By the fourth day, he was close to the border. Peter hid in a cluster of bushes about half a mile from it and observed the countryside. He could see the border and the peaceful farmhouses on the other side. From time to time a watchman passed slowly along the frontier on a bicycle. Then he saw two uniformed men on bicycles. A sense of apprehension and foreboding gripped Peter. As he feared, when they came opposite the bush in which he hiding, they stopped, put their bicycles down, and with their guns in hand, approached the bush. About ten feet from each other and twenty feet from the bush they stopped, guns ready.

"Prisoner of war, come out of your hiding!" they shouted arms over your in his direction. "Raise your hands. Do as you are told or we will shoot!"

To Peter it seemed like a dream, but he obeyed. He rose from the ground and with his hands raised moved toward the men. How could they have known? Only later did he learn that the entire population of the area had been alerted to watch for him, and that a farmer's wife, up and about early, had seen him disappear into the bush.

She had notified the authorities and the men had come to pick him up. At first his captors were strict and abrupt with Peter. But when he spoke to them in good German and they realized that he was quite harmless, they became friendlier. They even joked with him. At the next police station they handed him to their superiors and good-naturedly said good-bye over to him. The police delivered Peter to the military authorities in charge of all war prisoners for the region. They put him into a jail.

Most of the inmates turned out to be Russian prisoners of war who had somehow run afoul of the authorities. The majority had been working on some farm or project and had tried without success to escape. Now they were awaiting further developments. Some of them had already been questioned. They had been before the Colonel in charge of the camp. He was a strict disciplinarian, the prisoners said, but apparently reasonable and not unsympathetic to the prisoners. His interpreter was a corporal who spoke Russian well, was well informed about Russia and Russians and quite friendly to both.

Among the prisoners was also a fine specimen of a man, a Russian cavalry officer. As such they said, he should not have been detained with common soldiers, but the German commandant had put this man here to show his contempt for him. Along with other captured officers this man had been in camp for officers. These men, they said, were given special treatment. The calvary officer didn't have any special complaints, but he had asked the German authorities to assign some work to him. He couldn't bear to be idle, he had claimed. The Germans consented to appoint him an overseer over Russian war prisoners working on road construction provided he would give his word of honour - the word of a Russian officer, they said - that he would not attempt to flee or encourage his men to do so. The Russian gave his promise. A few weeks went by. Then one day the Russian officer with a number of his men deserted, but in vain. He and his men were soon captured and brought back to the German colonel to whom he had given the promise. For an officer to break his word of honour seemed to the German a despicable offense. Through his interpreter, Corporal Reinhard, the German officer informed the Russian that he considered him neither an officer nor a gentleman. He was an ordinary, despicable scoundrel, without any trace of honour. He despised such men. From then on he would be treated as an ordinary soldier, and a poor one at that. Thus he came to the soldiers' camp. The men that had deserted with him got away fairly easily. "Word of honour" obviously did not mean the same thing for Russian and German officers.

Eventually Peter Braun had to appear before the commandant too. An armed guard conducted him to the man's office. The colonel, a man of about sixty, sat behind his desk. At his side stood his interpreter, Corporal Reinhard, a man of about forty years. His name? Where was his home in Russia? When Peter named his home village, the interpreter asked him whether he was a Mennonite. Peter stared at the man. "Yes," he said. "I am a Mennonite."

"I know the Mennonites well," said the interpreter. "I attended the Zentralschule in Spat for three years and graduated from it. I like your people. Why did you try to desert, Braun? Have you been mistreated at the farm where you were placed?"

"No sir," replied Peter, "I was treated very well. I have no complaints. But I have been away from my loved ones for nearly two years and the longing for them was overpowering. I could not help myself, I had to try to get back to them." He spoke excellent German.

The colonel looked at Peter with compassion: "Poor young man. If I had been in your place I would likely have done the same thing. But you understand, Braun, we are at war. You are a prisoner of war and we cannot let you run away, even if we sympathize with you. For the time being you will return to your prison. You may see your fatherland sooner than you think. Dismissed." Peter was led away, but he felt much better than an hour earlier. The compassionate understanding of the officer had given Peter new courage and hope. But he puzzled about Corporal Reinhard.

Who was this man who knew the Mennonites and had attended a Mennonite *Zentralschule*?

In course of time the question was answered for him. Reinhard was a German of Lutheran persuasion. His parents, Russian subjects, had owned a small estate near Spat in the Crimea. He had attended and graduated from the Zentralschule in Spat. Later on, when he and his brother inherited their parent's estate, they began looking for a larger piece of property. Someone told them that with their money they could do well in eastern Germany. They went there and bought a large estate.

Their plans were to work this estate together for a few years and then buy a second property. They also acquired German citizenship. Soon thereafter the war with Russia broke out and Corporal Reinhard was drafted into the army while his older brother remained at home.

Since Reinhard spoke Russian fluently and knew Russia quite well, he was sent to intelligence school. Here he was taught the rudiments of the Russian military system and given other necessary information. Then he was sent to the front and put behind listen behind a listening apparatus by means of which he could hear what the Russians were saying in their trenches. Such information he had to write down. All along the front other men doing the same thing. The information was collected at a centre and evaluated. The Germans hoped that this information would give them insight into what was going on in Russia and what they planned to do.

After a time all the men with four children or more were freed from front line service. Reinhard too was sent back. He was appointed an interpreter for the commandant of all Russian war prisoners in the northeastern part of Germany. It was here that he met Peter Braun, the Mennonite from southern Russia.

More than two years had gone by since the day Peter Braun was taken prisoner by the Germans. He seldom heard from home and he knew little of what was going on in his fatherland. German newspapers were not always available to Peter and when some fell into his hands, it was clear that they were strictly censored and not too reliable.

In March, 1917, the news broke that the Russian Czar had been forced to abdicate and a new party had come into power in Russia. Germany rejoiced. The war-tired Germans hoped that this would be the end of the fighting, at least with the Russians. Peter heard what had happened but he had only a very hazy concept as to what this could mean for Russia. Like most Mennonites he was politically pretty naive and ill-informed. He knew though that during the war the Czarist government had been hostile to Russian citizens of German background and that it had planned to dispossess them and banish them to inhospitable regions in the north. He knew, moreover, that the great majority of the Russian people were very poor and were kept in ignorance, and that all the wealth and power was in the hands of a small strata in society. He knew that the orthodox church of Russia was very rich and had always made common cause with the government. That such conditions could not and should continue was clear to Peter. For this reason. he sympathized with the change in government, though to have it happen in the midst of a bloody and costly war caused him considerable misgiving. The future looked dark to him. He found it hard at such a momentous time to be far away from his fatherland and utterly unable to take part in what was going on.

Peter had been in Germany for over two years. Many things that he saw appealed to him, but it never even entered his mind to change his citizenship. He was surely a German, yet he preferred to think of himself as a Mennonite in an ethnic sense also and as a citizen of the mighty Russian empire. His family had been citizens there for more than a century. He was proud to be what he was. He had no desire to change anything. His one passion was to return home.

CHAPTER ELEVEN

RETURN TO THE FATHERLAND

It seemed that Providence was willing to fulfill his wish. Peter had asked to be sent back to the Mueller farm but instead he was told that in the near future he and his friends in the Red Cross units would be exchanged for German Red Cross workers captured by the Russians. His heart beat faster when he heard the news. In April, 1917, Peter was moved to another centre where he was reunited with his co-workers from Red Cross Train 189. They had been held prisoner in various places throughout Germany and each had his own story to tell. Now they were together again and filled with excitement. They were divided into three units, each to accompany a group of wounded Russians to their fatherland. Peter was in one of the three also.

Peter and eleven companions accompanied several hundred wounded Russians to their homeland. They travelled through Sweden and found it to be a beautiful country. The feelings of the men were mixed. Young and healthy when they left their homes, now they returned scarred. How would they be received? How would their families respond to them? How were they to make a living? These and similar thoughts weighed heavily on many of their minds. They belonged to various levels of Russian society and differed greatly in education and wealth, but all had one thing in common: they were returning home as cripples, unable to help themselves and dependent on other people.

The landscape they passed through was lovely. Local citizens knew about them and at nearly every station great masses of people had gathered to give them a rousing welcome. Orchestras played and they were showered with gifts and food. In the border city of Torino, in the extreme north, they were given a grand reception. Then the train rolled over the Russian frontier and towards Petrograd, later Leningrad. With great emotion, the men said, "This is our country, our fatherland!." Tears flowed down their cheeks as they sang,

> "For my home I am longing,
> In my home I'd like to be,
> Shone once so golden,
> There for me the sun of love."

The twelve Mennonites on the train all returned with their limbs intact. For nearly three years they had been away from their loved ones but none of them doubted they would be received with joy. As they travelled they tried to encourage their fellow returnees, but their own hearts were heavy too. They were Germans and they had heard that in Russia German-speaking citizens were being looked at askance. How would they be treated, what would be their destiny? Worrisome questions tugged at their minds.

Slowly the long train rolled into the Finnish Railway Station in Petrograd. Rousing music filled the air. The reception for them was as good as it possibly could have been and very moving. In the spacious train station they were served an excellent meal and then they were placed in fine automobiles and driven in triumph through the streets of the capital. The heroes had come home!

Finally they were taken to a hospital. Here the Mennonite men met the friends who had returned to their homeland earlier and whom they thought to be in their homes long ago. They heard from them that the authorities mistrusted all German soldiers and would not permit them to go home, fearing that they might make propaganda for Germany. The news hit the Mennonite men hard.

In the days that followed every one of the Mennonites were questioned closely. No accusations were brought against them, but they were not allowed to go home. The men appealed to various government departments and to influential public figures but no one seemed to be able to help them. Instead of going home, they were now sent to work on a railway line. Armed guards watched over them. Surrounded by the guards they were sent through the streets of the city to their place of work. The population watched them with hatred.

"German spies!" They shouted. "Kill them! Death to traitors! Death to all Germans!"

It seemed like a miracle that they were not torn to pieces right there on the street. Was this what they had come home to? Was this their "Fatherland'"?

The work they did was not too hard and in their lodging and in the hospital they were treated quite well. But they were closely guarded and obviously mistrusted. After some time the doctor in charge of the hospital told them that an investigation had fully cleared them and that they would be free in a few days. Representatives of the Mennonites who had taken up their cause were told the same thing: "Your men are innocent!" But instead of being set free the 37 Mennonite Red Cross workers were sent under military guard to Moscow, transported like ordinary criminals. In Moscow they were not taken to the headquarters of the Red Cross organization, as they expected, but to a prisoner of war camp. The commander of the camp, however, refused to accept them. These men were not prisoners of war and therefore did not come under his jurisdiction, he argued.

Negotiations began. Finally the commandant, a friendly man, spoke to the Mennonites. He would send them under military guard to the Biruljevo railway station where they would have to work on the line. They worked in Biruljevo for several weeks. There they to were allowed correspond with their families and Mennonite representatives visited them and pleaded their cause before the authorities. Finally, on July 3, the authorities decided that the Mennonites could be handed over to the Red Cross organization.

Though the order of release had been signed by the assistant to the Minister of War, the men were not handed back to the Red Cross. Their guards disappeared. The local population was friendly, but home leave was not granted to the men despite the fact that for more than three years they had not been home. They were still considered subversives. Russian citizens of German background learned during those years that they would never be accepted as full-fledged citizens by their adopted country, as long as they insisted on remaining what they were. These Germans - and there were about two million of them - had to choose between two possibilities: give up their language and identity and become part and parcel of the Russian nation, or leave the country. In the summer of 1918 this insight had just begun to dawn on these thirty-seven men, but in the years that followed they and their fellow Germans had to learn this lesson by hard experience.

Peter Braun and his fellow sufferers remained in reality - even if not officially - prisoners. But when the second revolution occurred in October and the Kerensky government was replaced, when anarchy boldly raised its ugly head in the great Russian Empire, when no party was able to assert itself and establish something resembling order, and when those who had oppressed them yesterday were suddenly themselves oppressed, the Mennonite men packed their things and without asking anyone's permission went wherever they wanted to go. Peter Braun decided to go home to Margenau where his parents and brothers and sisters, whom he had not seen for over three years, lived.

CHAPTER TWELVE

PETER COMES HOME

Peter had grown up in a quiet sober Mennonite village in the endless steppes of southern Russia. In those years he seldom got the opportunity to see a city and when he did he was greatly impressed. To get to a city as a teenager he and his father had to travel by railway and to Peter this had been a highlight of his life. He and his father always rode in a third class coach, which was clean and pleasant. The coach was divided into small eight passenger compartments. They had a good view of the landscape through which they were speeding. The passengers spoke a language which was different from the one he heard day in and day out in Margenau and seemed somehow very interesting. The conductor in his uniform too made quite an impression on the Mennonite village boy. And then the stations! They were truly impressive!

Before the Revolution the larger railway stations of Russia always had two waiting rooms. One was a first class room for the first and second class passengers. A porter in uniform stood at the door and admitted only passengers who in his opinion deserved to be in the room. Peter and his father, dressed in their Sunday best, were admitted. To Peter it seemed a splendid place. Passengers sat around, smoked and conversed; others sat at one of the many tables and white-liveried men served them tea or something else that they had ordered. Here as a teenager Peter saw a Russian lady pour cream into her tea. For Peter this was something totally new. At home they poured cream into their coffee, but into tea? He had not known that such a thing could be done.

There was also a large buffet. People stood in front of it and took tea from it or a bite to eat. To Peter they all seemed so sure of themselves and quite at home in this big and impressive room. He did not feel nearly so secure. In fact, he was so shy that had his father ordered tea, which he never did, Peter felt he could not have taken it here amongst all these fine people.

Since Peter had an inquisitive nature he usually also took a stroll through the other very large waiting room. Here he found the passengers who were travelling third and fourth class, who were quite a were different lot from the ones in the first class. He saw many peasants in their homespun clothing and high leather boots, labourers in dirty working clothes, soldiers, and also some quite well dressed farmers. The room was crowded and loud, the air full of cheap tobacco smoke. Here too was a buffet and people crowded before it as well. The room was not as impressive as the first one, but nevertheless Peter still found it interesting.

All this crowded back into Peter's mind as he with two companions arrived at one of the eleven Moscow railway stations to begin the trip south back to their homes. The station was overcrowded with people seeking railway passage; they stood and sat outside and inside the building. Trains, he found, were travelling irregularly. There were no porters at any of the doors nor was there any separation of first and second class. Everyone went where he wanted or was able to. The floors were unbelievably dirty. People sat and slept not only on the benches but also on the dirty floor.

The buffets were closed. Whenever a train pulled into the station the crowd simply rushed it. Although already overcrowded, new hundreds of passengers climbed into it. The aisles of the coaches were crowded right up to the doors and often passengers stood on the steps. Practically always there were many on the roof and others even rode on the buffers.

Many of these people would not listen to anyone. They travelled in groups and some of them were heavily armed. The war years had accustomed them to violence and cruelties; they swore fearfully and menaced anyone who dared to stand in their way. Peter Braun too had found two companions. They were not armed nor did they threaten anyone, but they stuck together for mutual protection. They had to squeeze themselves into the coach. Since stealing was the order of the day, one of them watched over luggage other two searched for food or attended to other things.

Finally Peter arrived at his destination, the Stuljnevo station. He found a Russian peasant who agreed to take him to his native village. Peter put his things on the dilapidated wagon and the peasant forced his skinny horses into a slow trot. It was quiet here. Autumn had arrived but there was still no snow on the ground. The plowed fields stretched away to the horizon. From where they drove Peter could see a number of well-organized Mennonite villages. From a distance they looked like oases in a desert. The large farm buildings lay surrounded by spreading trees and gardens. Many of the roofs were covered with red bricks and they conveyed to the viewer a feeling of warmth and cosiness. It was a peaceful scene. But from what the peasant was saying it was clear that life around here was not as quiet as it appeared to be. The waves created by the revolution had reached this secluded place too.

Just before Margenau Peter asked the man to stop. He wanted to observe the village from here for a while. It lay before him in a slight hollow; stretched out, orderly and peaceful. He could see people walking on the street and hear roosters crowing. It was his native village! How he loved this place and how he had longed to see it! He hoped that here he would be able to forget all the bitterness of the last few years. They drove on into the village and into his parents' yard. The yard was empty. Peter put his things on the porch before the door of the house and told the coachman that he could unharness his horses and feed them. The front door opened and his mother came out of the house. Surprised, she looked at the soldier standing in front of her. Then she took a closer look and exclaimed: "Peter! My son! Is it really you? Have you really come home?"

With a leap Peter mounted the porch. Mother and son embraced wordlessly. Their hearts were too full for words. Then she pushed her son back.

"Let me look at you, Peter," she said. She looked directly into her eldest son's face, and examined him closely: "Have you come home healthy and unspoiled my son?"

"Yes Mother," Peter replied, "I'm still healthy and I'm very much as I was when I left you; I'm only older and I now carry a wound in my heart. The depressing prisoner of war camp and the disgraceful, dishonourable reception given us by Russia, the country that is supposed to be our fatherland, have hurt me, Mother. They've hurt me very badly, but I hope to recover here and become well again."

Mrs. Braun took her son by the hand. "Come in, Peter," she said. "We didn't know you were coming - Father has gone visiting. Your brother Jakob is, as far as we know, on the Caucasian front. Your sisters are at home and they'll be glad to see you."

In the kitchen Peter met his sister Kathe, now eighteen years old. When he had last seen her she had been a teenager, but now she was a beautiful young woman. Kathe greeted her eldest brother, whom she had always greatly admired, with enthusiasm. She found it very romantic to think of him as a soldier and prisoner of war. She kissed him warmly. Anna, the baby of the family, who had once brought the letter calling Peter to the service, and was now fourteen years old, too greeted him impetuously. Both girls had great admiration for their oldest brother, who stood before them in the flower of manhood.

Then Anna rushed through the backdoor. She knew where her father was. He had to share in their happiness and Anna wanted to be the first to bring him the joyous news of his eldest son's return.

Farmer Braun was visiting with a neighbor Hiebert, the way Mennonite farmers had habit of doing in fall when their field and garden labours were completed. Men sat together and talked about their farms, the village news, what had transpired in their congregation, about their Russian neighbors and the uncertain times they were living in. They compared information about their sons who had been taken from them to serve in faraway places and spoke of other things. Braun and Hiebert had grown up together; when they were youngsters they had played together, and had been to public school together. They knew each other as well as it is possible to know another person. To them it was a pleasure to be together even when there was nothing to talk about. But in those evil, uncertain years there was always something to talk or complain about.

Anna rushed into the room leaving the door wide open behind her. "Father," she exclaimed. "Father, our Peter is home! He has just arrived. Come home, Father. Oh, our Peter has become such a fine fellow! Let's go, Father!"

It seemed as if the old man did not first comprehend what his daughter was saying. ""What are you saying, child? Peter at home? How can that be possible? Then I must go immediately. Good-bye, Hiebert." And he left as fast as his feet could carry him. Anna took his hand and walked with him up to the boundary of their property. Then she let go of her father's hand and ran into the house.

The elder Braun followed his daughter into the house. Peter stood in the front room. The father did not say much. "Have you come home, Peter? Thank God!" Then he embraced his son.

During the next few days only those chores were attended to at the Brauns that could not be postponed. The family needed all the time to relate what had occurred during the long years of separation. Neighbors and friends arrived to welcome Peter and to hear from him at least something of what he had experienced. He had to tell his story over and over again. All were worried and depressed to learn that the returning Mennonite prisoners of war had been imprisoned in their homeland. That simply meant that they were looked upon as strangers and were mistrusted. It was clear to them that two groups existed in Russia, the one who valued the contributions the Mennonites and Germans were making to the development of the country and the other, led by the *Slavophiles*[*], the self-styled "genuine Russians," who did not. These people hated all strangers and all those who did not speak Russian or did not belong to the ruling Orthodox Church.

They talked about the new government though they knew little of it. The names Lenin and Trotsky had already filtered into

---

* A *Slavophile* is one who greatly admires the Slavic people, their institutions, and their art.

the Mennonite colonies. But who were these men? No one knew from before. It was known that these men headed a party known as "Bolsheviks", that the party favored the confiscation of all private property, and that it advocated the replacement of old morals, of marriage and of the old social concepts with new and strange sounding ones. No one knew exactly what the party stood for, but what they heard sounded so fantastic that they were reluctant to believe it. If these new rulers really attempted to turn everything upside down, they felt Western Europe would interfere and declare a crusade against them. It seemed a logical conclusion, but these farmers did not as yet know what the astute student of human nature, Lenin, had replied when the same objection had been made to the plans proposed by him. He had reportedly said, "Never fear, comrades. We shall give the Western capitalists a chance to make some profits through these revolutionary changes. Then they won't bother us because these capitalists are always ready to commit suicide for a profit."

CHAPTER THIRTEEN

PETER AT HOME

Peter's family showed him pictures of his brother Jakob who was serving in a Red Cross ambulance corps at the Caucasian front. He had been in this service for nearly two years. From time to time Jakob had been home on leave. His family repeated what he had said about the various nations living in the Caucasian mountains. These warlike mountaineers were mostly of the Islamic religion; they spoke their own languages and had a lifestyle completely different from the Russians. The region they were living in was very picturesque, with steeply forbidding mountains and lovely, often very fertile, valleys between them.

The Russian army had invaded Turkey and Jakob's corps had followed the army. He had many interesting stories to tell about the population of that region. On one occasion their army had pushed the Turks back a considerable distance. The population had fled before the advancing Russians. The Red Cross train had stopped near a deserted Turkish village. There someone had found a little child, a girl, likely left behind in the panic by her parents. She was a healthy and beautiful child, but with a different beauty from that of the Mennonite children. Her skin was an olive colour, she had a narrow eagle nose, black eyes and black hair. What were they do with the child? They had no alternative but to keep her and so the men looked after the little girl and in time came to love her. She became the darling of the corps.

Later one of the Mennonite men obtained the consent of his wife to bring the child to his home and to adopt the little Turk as their own daughter. When the man went home on leave he took the child with him and so a Turkish girl came to grow up in a Mennonite village. In the future someone will likely wonder how the features of a mountain people of the Caucasian region came into a family of German-Dutch Mennonites.

Kathe, Peter's sister, had graduated from the Gnadenfeld *Maedchenschule* (Girls School). She was now assisting her mother in the house and garden. She liked housekeeping and she was a lover of books, a trait she shared with her brother Peter. When Peter in a big brotherly fashion wanted to know if she had a boyfriend, Kathe tossed her head back and replied that she was not thinking of such matters. But the teasing glance of her eyes contradicted her words. Her eyes suggested that she had given this matter a good deal of attention and that her thoughts had taken a quite definite direction. As they bantered back and forth, Peter recalled an experience he once had. While swimming in the nearby brook he had pulled a little boy, Henry Penner, the son of a local farmer, out of a water hole. Just for fun he had asked the dripping boy of about ten years:

"Well, Henry, whom do you plan to marry someday?"

Without hesitation the little fellow had shot back,

"Your sister Kathe!"

Peter had found his spontaneous reply quite amusing at that time. Recalling it now, on an intuition he asked Kathe:

"Say, Kathe, where is the Henry Penner who is about two years older than you are? Is he still around?"

Kathe's cheeks reddened slightly. "What makes you think of him, Peter?" she inquired.

"No special reason, Kathe." Peter said, "It was just that I was reminded of him. Possibly because he was such a quick, self-assured little fellow."

Kathe laughed. She knew the story of the waterhole and Henry's reply. Without betraying any special interest she reported that Henry had been assisting his father on the farm in the summers and in winter had attended the *Kommerzschule* (School of Commerce) in Halbstadt. A year ago he too had been mobilized and now was serving in a military office in Kiev.

"And what about Anna, the baby of the family?" Peter asked. He was told that Anna had graduated from the public school and had attended the Maedchenschule in Gnadenfeld for a term. At present she was a second term student there. It so happened that she was at home for a few days.

Peter's father and mother had aged somewhat, he found, but not too much. Father and the girls looked after the farm. They kept a labourer if possible, though as things now stood labourers were not always available. For this reason, Peter's father had to work harder than was good for him. At present they had a Russian teenager working for them. The youth looked after the animals though he had to be supervised closely because he was in the habit of forgetting things.

Peter inspected the barn and garden. He found that the farm was in good shape, though possibly not quite as good as when he still was at home. Yet it was obvious that this yard was under good management.

CHAPTER FOURTEEN

LENA WALL

They talked about Peter's friend Peter Klassen and his tragic death in the waters of the Black Sea. During the last three years Peter had seen many people die and many tragedies, but the untimely death of his friend affected him deeply. Peter asked about John Wiens. What did they know about him? They reported that he had returned from service because of a weak heart and married some girl in his village. That was about all they knew of John Wiens. Peter had a desire to see John but an even greater desire to see Lena Martens. No one in his family knew anything about her since he had never mentioned her to them. He had received one postcard from her at the beginning of his imprisonment in Germany, but that was all. Now he didn't even know whether she was still alive or not. He must see her, he decided, but first he would have to write to her. Though the mail by now was very bad, he had to risk it. So he wrote Lena.

About a month later the mail brought Peter a letter. He could see that it was from Lena. The sight of the letter so excited him that he could not open it immediately. Peter had a feeling that the letter contained bad news for him. When he finally overcame his hesitation, his intuition was confirmed. It read:

Neu-Halbstadt, February 23, 1918.

Dear Friend Peter Braun:

I received your rather unexpected letter on January 6th. I am glad to hear that you are alive and well, and at home with your parents. About two years ago I heard from you briefly for the last time through a postcard from a prisoners' camp in Germany. We got to know each other about three and half years ago. I found you attractive and I was interested in you, but we've never had more than a pleasant friendship as occurs quite often between young people. After you left to serve in the army, we wrote frequently at first and you sent me your photo. Then you were captured by the enemy. From then on I heard from you very seldom and when I did it was only an open card with the few words permitted a prisoner of war. Your memory began to fade.

A little over a year ago a young man was engaged to teach in our village school. He too had been serving in the army and as a teacher was discharged. We got to know each other. He wooed me. My parents wanted us to be married and I too liked the young man. Three months ago we had our wedding and I am now Mrs. Frank Wall.

At first I didn't know whether I should answer your letter. But then I felt honour bound to inform a dear friend of how things are. I am happy with Frank and I love him. I am sure you two would like each other too if you ever met. My husband has read this letter and he sends you his best wishes. Both of us invite you to visit us if you can make it possible. It is my wish that you too might find someone with whom you could be as happy as I am with my dear husband.

Very sincerely,

Lena Wall.

Peter read the letter to its end, his senses slowly comprehending what it said. This much was clear: Lena was married and he had to forget her. His friend Peter was dead. In Germany he had been an alien, and in Russia, his so-called Fatherland, he too was classified as an alien and suspected of being a foreign spy. A great void – a terrible loneliness - seemed to engulf him. He could not blame Lena. She was not obligated to him. In fact, he had himself insisted, when they parted, that both remain free. She had acted honourably by answering his letter as she had done. All this he freely admitted, but he was still terribly lonely.

CHAPTER FIFTEEN

THE GERMAN OCCUPATION

The political situation in southern Russia was worsening every day. For the time being there were no troubles in Peter's native village Margenau. Situated as it was middle of the large Mennonite settlement, it enjoyed a tranquility alien to most places in the Ukraine. But disquieting rumors were everywhere. The villages on the edge of the settlement were being raided by bandits, first at night but lately by day. These bandits robbed the farm yards and took wagons and horses and anything else they wanted. So far there was no open violence, although in larger places, especially in the cities of the country, a great deal of blood was flowing. Brother was killing brother.

Then on February 17, 1918, in the Molotschna settlement this all changed. On that day six Mennonites were shot in Helbstadt, among them two teachers of the local Kommerzschule, Hausknecht and Peter Letkemann, and the well-known estate owner Jakob Sudermann. They were murdered without the benefit of any court. Besides them, a boy of sixteen and a young man of eighteen years were also murdered. This was done by a bloodthirsty band who had descended upon the town and proclaimed themselves the representatives of the new government. Unprecedented robbing now began. Stationed in the nearby town of Tokmak was a band of cutthroats. On stolen horses, armed to the teeth, they rode through the neighboring Mennonite villages. No one was safe from them. From Tokmak they caroused, plundered and murdered. The called themselves the "Red Guard." Three young men of Mennonite parents, all sons of poor families, joined this band, very much against the wish of their families. Two of the fellows were from the village of Ladekop, Johann Wiebe and Abram Friesen, and the third man was a Kroeker.

A shudder of horror went through the 57 Mennonite villages in the Molotschna settlement. What had happened in Halbstadt could be repeated at any time and anywhere. No one was safe. Peter Braun could stand the strain no longer. He wanted someone to speak to and someone who might have answers for his many questions. He decided to go to Halbstadt, the colony's cultural centre, where he had a cousin with whom he could stay for a fortnight. To be in Halbstadt was more dangerous than to be in Margenau, but Peter was willing to take the risk. A neighbor with some business in the towm took Peter with him and the cousin was glad to have Peter stay in his home for some time.

The cousin and his wife told him about the many details gruesome events that had occurred in Halbstadt. One day Peter went to visit the highschool teacher Franz Janzen, whom he had learned to know in Petrograd. Janzen was a well-educated, informed and interesting man. A graduate of the Petrograd University, he had served during the war in some office in that city. Whenever possible he had participated in the city's cultural life, and due to his wide interests he had made many friends and established valuable contacts with leading personalities. When the Mennonite Red Cross soldiers were put in detention in Petrograd, Janzen visited them, assisted them in various ways and used his contacts to help them. Peter respected this man and was confident that he would enlighten him on many things.

The Janzen home stood on a side street in Halbstadt. Like most Mennonite houses it was some distance from the street. Between the sidewalk and the Janzen property ran a wooden painted fence. On the property and along the street stood a row of old, mighty acacia trees. Before the house was a well-tended flower garden, practically obligatory for Mennonite homes in Russia. There were high trees around the house and fruit trees and decorative shrubs in the garden. The entire setting reflected good stewardship and conveyed a sense of peace.

Franz Janzen greeted Peter at the door and took him into the house and introduced him to his wife. Mrs. Janzen was a lively and pleasant woman. She was a graduate of the Women's Gymnasium of Berdjansk and had taught a few years before their marriage. Both husband and wife spoke fluent German and Russian and had a working knowledge of French as most Russian intellectuals had. Their many books in these three languages witnessed to the fact that the couple enjoyed reading.

On the walls were photos of famous German and Russian writers and also a few paintings. Among them Peter recognized "Prince Ivan on a Gray Wolf" by Wasnezov, the original of which he had seen in the Tretjakov Art Gallery in Moscow, and also one by the Mennonite painter Johann Janzen. Peter liked the home and its inhabitants.

Janzen, the teacher, was not only well educated and well read, he was also one of those individuals who take a lively interest in what is going on in the world. Peter found it a pleasure to discuss his concerns with this man.

Unavoidably they discussed first the tragedy that had occurred in Halbstadt. The Janzens reported that very few of the bandits terrorizing the town were local. The labourers of Halbstadt and Tokmak condemned such activities and had no share in them. They favored the revolution and desired a more equal distribution of property, but this wanton destruction and murder they disapproved of. At present even the labourers were not absolutely safe. When the eight Mennonites were murdered, an eighteen-year-old Russian youth, the son a labourer, condemned these excesses. The bandits shot him too. The worst elements in the country, heavily armed and lusting to give full rein to their insatiable and sadistic cravings, controlled the situation, and woe to anyone standing in their way.

Franz Janzen said that a revolution in Russia had been unavoidable. The Czarist government did not crumble because of a revolutionary assault from without, it crashed to the ground because of its own weakness. When the collapse came there was no intelligent, effective leadership from above in Russia. The peasants were backward, illiterate and totally unable to express a political will. The majority of the upper classes did not understand the demands of the time. They were old-fashioned reactionaries, whose greatest desire was to restore the vast estates to their former owners and maintain the status quo.

Janzen, when he was still in Petrograd, had listened to Lenin and Trotzky many times. Lenin, he said, was a capable and intelligent man with a burning thirst for power. He had the courage to act or halt as the situation demanded and a fierce conviction of the rightness of his cause. combined with an ability to simplify the issues and appeal to the masses. Plain in his dress and appearance, he was the man that gave the prostrate nation the leadership it otherwise lacked. Thus, he made himself the ruler of the country. Lenin and his small but disciplined group of followers never hesitated to do what they felt would promote their cause, making themselves the rulers and the spokesmen for the nation, despite the fact that the great majority of the nation never asked them to be their rulers. Trotsky, more mercurial than Lenin, too was a very capable man and a superb organizer.

Peter Braun remained in Halbstadt in the home of his relatives, the Fasts. At that time radio was unheard of and newspapers were unavailable, thus the population was forced to rely on rumours passed from mouth for their information. The fact that these were often contradictory in nature did not prevent them from spreading from town to town and village to village. Rumours had it that the Germans would occupy the Ukraine. The bandits, styling themselves the government, contradicted these rumours and threatened death to anyone repeating them. In spite of that they persisted.

One lovely April day, Peter was busying himself with some work in the Fast house while Mrs. Fast was away. After a time she returned in great excitement. "Peter," she said, "big things are happening. Our tormentors have suddenly disappeared. Not single one is in sight. They say that the Germans will occupy our town within an hour or so. People are rushing to the railway depot."

The news sounded strange to Peter but he immediately left the house. Walking along the main street he noticed the excitement of the townspeople. They were standing in groups on the sidewalk or even in the middle of the street. Many were walking in the direction of the railway station. He went there too.

At the station a substantial number of people were standing around and appeared to be waiting for something. Peter noticed that there were no Russians among this group, only Mennonites and a few Germans from nearby Prishib. Tables were brought and set up on the platform; and as if by magic coffee and cookies and other goods appeared. Mennonite girls stood behind the tables ready to serve. Peter marvelled.

A train slowly approached. Soldiers in German uniform stood on the locomotive. When the train came to a halt, German soldiers filled the platform. They ate at the canteen and admired the girls with their "lovely thick calves" as they put it. Everything went smoothly and in an orderly way, until something happened that shocked many of those present, especially the women and the and children. Three prisoners, well-known bandits and murderers, were brought forward from one of the coaches and shot in sight of everybody. Peter and most of those present felt like this was a poor choice of time and place, even if the men were murderers. After all, they were Russians and they were being shot by German invaders in a town populated by Germans. The Germans said they had come to stay. The Ukraine would be occupied by them for fifteen years; the nightmare for the local population had come to an end. Everything would be normal again, but Peter was not convinced. He had an uneasy feeling, a foreboding that the future would not be as rosy as painted by the Germans. He decided to stay in Halbstadt for few a more days and then to return to his native village.

In the days that followed the Germans arrested a few of the men who had cooperated with the Red Guards. These fellows had been in hiding but had been betrayed by their enemies. Not all of those arrested were wicked men; really some had done no more than to sympathize with the revolution, though not with the bandits. As always happens in such a time, there were those who likely wanted to square old accounts and denounced those who had mistreated them to the Germans. Mennonite leaders intervened for such men and in most cases were able to obtain their release. In some instances they even intervened for genuine bandits and occasionally, though not always, freed them too. Later many of the intercessors had reason to question whether they had been wise to intervene on behalf of these bandits. When these spared fellows were free again and the Germans left they went about their business of torturing and murdering people with renewed vigor.

Before the coming of the Germans, the forces then in power had ordered the well-to-do farmers – including most of the Mennonites – to hand over a certain amount of horses, cattle, wagons and farm machinery to the poor of to the neighboring Russian villages. When the Germans came to villages, they ordered this property to be returned to their rightful owners. Many owners too demanded their property back. Later on they had to pay for this. But there were individual Mennonite farmers and even whole villages who refused to take their things back, or who at least came to a friendly understanding with the persons who had taken their goods.

The forces of occupation naturally wanted to establish as many safe areas as possible and support themselves with them. The German villages in Russia, of which there were hundreds, seemed ready made for this purpose. A propaganda campaign began. The German citizens of Russia, who for years had been accused of sympathizing with the Germans, who had been called spies and traitors at the same time their sons were dying on the battlefields for Russia, whom the government had intended to dispossess and to banish into the inhospitable regions of the north, whose homes and farms had been robbed, whose men had been murdered and women raped, these people were now very vulnerable for this propaganda. The Mennonites too remembered that they were Germans. A spirit of nationalism lifted its head among them and hand in hand with it spirit of militarism. People were encouraged to take measures to protect themselves from the bandits. In order to protect themselves it was necessary for them to arm themselves. No one spoke of assisting the Germans; even they never proposed that this should be done, they spoke only of self-protection against roving bands of bandits. Men who had seen their women folk being raped were quite susceptible to such a line of thinking.

When Peter returned to Margenau he found that nothing special had happened there and superficially it seemed as if things were back to normal again. But he was worried. He had lived in Germany for a time and he had seen the people as they were. He felt that his fellow villagers had a totally wrong impression of the Germans. Not even one in a thousand had been to Germany. They knew that country and its people only from the readers they were using in the schools. In them the Germans naturally appeared at their best. The often naïve Mennonites and Germans of Russia took it for granted that all Germans were as those described in these book: honest, pure, hard-working and God-fearing.

Peter remembered the experience of an eighteen year old youth of Margenau who had come to the Apostolovo railway station. There he had bought a paper printed in Germany - the first he had ever seen. He was thrilled. Among other things the paper contained a story told as a joke. The anecdote related that there was a writer whose wife had a tablecloth with the inscription: "A cheerful guest is always welcome!" She gave the tablecloth to her maid. A few days later the girl's bed was graced with a bedspread - the former tablecloth - announcing in bold letters: "A cheerful guest is always welcome!"

The young Mennonite was bitterly disappointed. From his childhood he had heard dirty jokes by the dozen from their family's Russian workers. But that, he felt, was done by illiterate Russian peasants who didn't know any better. But to learn that the Germans were in this respect no better was for this young man a bitter disillusionment. Many Germans in Russia idealized the citizens of Germany. Peter could see the harm that would result. He was told that the German military were organizing various festivities in Halbstadt, such as the Ludendorf Festivals, where beer flowed. Mennonite girls, unfamiliar with the superficially polite forms and easy manners the flatteries of the western Europe, were not immune to young Germans. They did not escape unscathed.

The security provided by the Germans lasted only a short time. In October they had to evacuate the Ukraine. The Russian citizens of German descent were left to their fate. Everybody feared what they knew was to come. Terror was in the air. And not without reason. Countless armed bands appeared again if by magic. They tyrannized the population. Isolated farms and small settlements were overrun. Torture, robbing, raping and murder became the pastime of these bandits. Those that could left their homes in terror and fled to the larger settlements. In practically every Mennonite village of the Molotschna settlement there now lived a number of families who until recently had been well-to-do and, in many cases, rich estate or factory owners. They had left their property behind and come to the Molotschna settlement for safety. They had shocking stories to tell of what had happened to their friends and neighbors who had not fled while it was still possible to do so.

But there were also stories of courage and self sacrifice. One concerned a Bergen family whose home was overrun by a group of bandits. They demanded to be fed and then searched the home, taking what they pleased and not overlooking a single room from the basement to the attic. The family had two girls, one seventeen and the other nineteen years old. The father, Jakob Bergen, knew only too well the danger his daughters were in and remained as close to them as he could. When he heard a sob in an adjacent room he went to where the sound came from. There stood the girls and in front of them two fellows with drawn revolvers. "What is the matter, girls? Why are you crying?" asked the father.

"These men demand that we submit to them. If not they threaten to shoot us!"

"Children, it is better to die in honour than to live in disgrace!'" said the father.

All this was spoken in Low German which the bandits could not understand. They demanded of Bergen that he repeat in Russian what he had said to his daughters. The father faced the bandits fearlessly and said: "I am the father of these girls and I am advising them to die rather than submit to your disgraceful demand!"

The men leaped toward Bergen and pulled him into the next room. The girls were forgotten for the moment. They used the few seconds of grace and escaped unnoticed to safety. The two bandits put Bergen against a wall and pointed a revolver at his face, making fun at him. Other bandits in the room soon joined in too. They seemed to be having a good time. Then one of the bandits pressed a trigger and shot Bergen in the left cheek, the bullet leaving his head behind the left ear. Blood flowed from the wounded man's face and he began to walk. The bandits made way for him. Bergen walked through two rooms filled with men. They let him pass expecting him to drop at any time. But when Bergen reached the yard, one of the men watching him called out: "Give him another one or he may get away!" At that instant Bergen jumped over the fence and ran into the garden. Bullets whizzed over his head as he escaped with his life. The wound healed in time though Bergen was deaf on his left ear.

CHAPTER SIXTEEN

NON-RESISTANCE TESTED

For some time the question of non-resistance had been on Peter's mind. He knew that the refusal to carry weapons, to serve in the army, and to defend oneself against attackers had from the beginning been one of the tenets of the Mennonite faith. But was this tenet still valid at a time when chaos ruled the land and decent citizens trembled for their property, honour and life and when wicked people committed indescribable atrocities? Was the Mennonite brotherhood following an impossible dream when it insisted on total non-resistance? How had this teaching stood up in times of trial? Did Mennonite history have no illustrations of such moments in its past?

Peter decided to visit the village school teacher Kasdorf, one of the few men in the village interested in the history of his people and familiar with it. Teacher Kasdorf willingly entered into the discussion, at Peter's request, and related two incidents which could shed light on the problems the Mennonites now faced.

In 1880 a group of Mennonites left their comfortable homes in southern Russia and trekked eastward to seek asylum from service in the government forestry camps. Because of their non-resistant stance they felt that such service would be a compromise of their faith. After great a number of hardships these settlers eventually established two settlements on the Amu-Darje river in Central Asia in the midst of a Muslim population. These people, the Jamudes, were very friendly during the day, but at night they stole the horses of the settlers. One of the two settlements engaged a few Russian Cossacks as guards. This stopped all thieving. The second settlement took the position that the hiring of armed guards was a violation of Mennonite non-resistance tenets and accused the first of lack of faith. But now the second settlement was losing more and more of their valuable horses. Secretly, these settlers too to began guard their horses. One of their young men, Heinrich Abrahams, had recently married.

One night bandits broke into his house and murdered the young husband. The wife fled through a window and narrowly escaped her would-be abductors. From then on thieving and breaking into homes became frequent. The young men of the village wanted to defend their families but the fathers categorically forbade it. In the end, however, robberies became so frequent and threatening that the villagers finally defended them selves. Reality forced them to abandon their cherished principle of non-resistance, in practice if not in theory. Eventually they left the dangerous place; about twenty families went the to Canada and the rest went elsewhere.

In 1901 the Mennonites of Russia bought for their landless a large area of land in the Terek region on which they established 17 villages. These villages were surrounded by half-wild Muslim neighbors. Robbing and stealing with these people was an ancient tradition and to some of the tribes even an honourable occupation. As long as the Czarist government was in power the people were kept more or less in check, although there always was some stealing and several of the Mennonites were murdered too. But when the

Czarist government fell, the settlers were left without protection. The two groups, the church Mennonites and the Mennonite Brethren met in a common brotherhood meeting to discuss the proposal. The majority vote went against it.

By now the settlers were being robbed wholesale; hundreds of their horses and cattle were being tken. Bandits broke into their homes, blood flowed and women were raped. The young men tried to fight back. Bandits were shot and some of the Mennonite men lost their lives too. The traditional non-resistant stance simply had not survived in the face of reality.

How did the episode end? All the villages and all that they owned there had to be abandoned. The Terek settlers were glad to escape with their lives. Acting in self-defence likely saved them from many outrages that the Muslims might have committed. No matter what their attitude would have been, the end would have been the same: they would have had to flee. The native people hated the Russian settlers; they were much more friendly to the Germans and the Mennonites. But they looked upon Europeans and all Christians as intruders and, therefore, people they had every right to rob and mistreat. It appears, said Kasdorf, that non-resistance could not survive in the face of reality.

CHAPTER SEVENTEEN

SOUL SEARCHING IN THE MOLOTSCHNA

The fifty-seven Mennonite villages of the Molotschna settlement had to make a decision: should they bow before these bandits and allow them to do whatever came into their minds or should they organize and protect themselves? They had been put into a position of undreamed-of difficulty. There was no government that could give them protection no matter how outrageous the acts perpetrated against them. At that very moment they were threatened by the most ruthless criminals and bandits. Everything they held dear, their property, their homes. the honour of their women and their very life, was at stake. What should they do? Submit? Resist?

From the end of June to the beginning of July a conference of all churches had already been held in Lichtenau where a consensus to the question of resistance had been sought but not found.

Such questions are hardly ever answered by the majority, they are resolved by an energetic minority. In the Molotschna settlement too various minority groups came forward with answers. Some were in favor of arming themselves for protection and others for absolute non-resistance. A bitter struggle between the groups ensued. Tolerance was forgotten - if it had ever existed. The bi-weekly paper *Die Friedensstimme* which appeared again during these months, brought an article by B.B. Janz in which he warned the Mennonite people not to arm and advised them to rely on God for protection. In the heat of the debate and because of their great fear his warning was not heeded.

Representatives of the villages were called to a meeting in in Rueckenau to discuss the situation and come to some consensus. The meeting was dominated by the group in favour of resistance. However, a representative of the village of Rosenort, Peter Bergmann, a respected citizen, spoke to the assembly and warned them not to arm. "Seek God's help and protection," he pleaded. He cited instances from the past when God had helped. "God," Bergmann said, "can do it again." Those in favour of resistance shouted: "Throw him out! Out with him!" The meeting ended without a decision.

A second meeting was called in Gnadenfeld. Here David Janzen, a minister of the church Mennonites and a citizen of the village of Rudnerweide, warned the delegates against self-defense. "Put your trust in God," he cried. "He can and will help."

"Spit into his face!" they shouted. Many of those present actually believed as Janzen did, yet not one stood by him with even one word.

The leading men of the Mennonite Brethren church in Alexandertal were opposed to resistance. On Sunday their minister, Heinrich Goossen, spoke a sermon from Isaiah 59:1-2: *"Behold, the Lord's hand is not shortened, that it cannot save, or his ear dull, that it cannot hear; but your iniquities have made a separation between you and your God, and your sins have hidden his face from you so that he does not hear."*

On the following Tuesday there was meeting of the Villagers of Alexandertal. A German-speaking officer, a non-Mennonite, had been invited to the meeting and was also asked to be the chairman. The weeds have to be destroyed, he said – the Mancho men were worse than weeds Goossen was publicly criticized for his sermon on Sunday and told: "We will put you before a court of *White** officers and shoot you like a dog." No one protested.

But many people, even if they did not speak up when they should have, clung to the principle of non-resistance and refused to be armed. Two villages took this position, one of these the orthodox village of Pastwa. It could not be said that members of one Mennonite church took one position and those of another a different one. The conflict cut across the groups. Nor could it be proved that it was only ruffians like the chairman of the meeting in Alexandertal who favoured resistance; among those in favour were also respected and gentle men. They saw the bestial deeds that were being committed - torture of innocent people, murders and the fearful rapes of young girls and old women and they honestly believed that it was their duty to prevent such outrages, no matter what the cost. They cited the Bible: Abraham had armed his servants to save Lot; David had killed Goliath; Samson the Philistines. Refugees from devastated villages related how their sisters and daughters had been gang raped before their very eyes, and many a woman or young girl wept bitterly because of what she had been through. In face of such situations, many men felt they had no choice. It was a determined minority, and not necessarily an un-Christian and unthinking one who decided to arm The majority followed, though with a heavy heart. All they wanted was to protect their villages, but soon it was argued that the best protection was not defence but offence.

---

* The *White Army* was the name given to the pro-Czarist coalition.

CHAPTER EIGHTEEN

THE FIRST BLOODY ENCOUNTER

December 10, 1918. An alarm is signalled in Halbstadt. Young armed men from all parts of the town, though mainly students of the Kommerzschule, are rushing to the meeting place in front of the to Volost office.

The German sergeant-major, Sonntag, is in command. The men are informed that the *Machno** bands have occupied the Russian village of Tschernigovka, and as a result the two adjacent Mennonite villages of Sparau and Kontiniusfeld are in mortal danger. The Halbstadt men are to go to the help of these villages. Having received their orders the men line up, turn right and march to the railway station. They sing:

"*Muss i denn, muss i denn
zum Städtele hinaus, Städtele hinaus,
Und du, mein Schatz, bleibst hier?
Wenn i komm', wenn i komm'*"

---

* *Nestor Machno* was an anarchist revolutionary, and his followers were known as the *Machnovzy,*

("Must I, then, must I, then
to the village must I then, village must I then,
And thou, my dear, stay here?
When I'm back, when I'm back.")

Youth doesn't worry and has little respect for danger.

At the station, a locomotive and a single car are ready for departure. One hundred and ten men squeeze into the car, overfilling it as it leaves. They arrive at the Waldheim railway station and empty out of the coach. It is dark for now. The young men have to spend the night in the station building, where they are met by leading men from the Gnadenfeld Defence Centre. A plan of action is explained. The Halbstadt men will attack Tschernigovka from one end, the men from Gnadenfeld from the right and the local cavalry under Gerhard Toews from the left. The village is to be attacked simultaneously from all sides.

Early in the morning the marching line reaches the village. The village is about two kilometers long, though only a hundred meters wide. All seems to be quiet. They meet few villagers and are told that there are no strangers in the village. The line moves on until it reaches the square before the church. People are coming out of the church. An old man approaches the Mennonites - one he likely knows - and offers him a piece of cake blessed by the priest, whispering a warning as he does: *"The Machno band are expecting you. Beware!"*

At that moment a Halbstadt man shoots at a bothersome dog. Immediately bullets whizz from all sides. Some distance away mounted men appear. The Mennonites hug the ground and return the fire. A rider drops from his horse. From the church tower and the windmill the men are shot at, until a few well-aimed bullets silence the guns. The Mennonites jump up, run forward again. A student, John Martens, is hit in the head and dies instantly. The gun falls out of his hands, the body makes one grotesque motion, then, face up, lies still. Martens' blood sprays the face of the man next to him, Abram Friesen. On the other side, lying close to him is his brother. When he sees what has happened he raises himself and kisses his dead brother. Then he grabs his gun and with the others rushes forward.

The Machnovzy have had enough; they but are eager to retreat but finding it difficult. A number of the bandits take refuge in a yard surrounded by heavy stone wall and defend themselves stubbornly. A German soldier, Sergeant Henschel, ties a few hand grenades together and throws them over the fence. A bullet hits him in the head and kills him instantly. A young Matties is shot through the hand while a student is wounded. Now the Machovzy are running. They have lost heavily. They are not fighting for a principle but for the loot and lusts they can satisfy. Few people are willing to risk their lives for such a reason, though a few among them do defy danger. Peter Braun sees one bandit kneeling in the open street and firing at the approaching line until a bullet sends him crumbling to the ground. The Mennonites are inexperienced and not too well organized. The Gnadenfeld men did not attack when they should have. There had been arguments among them. Somewere not even willing to attack, all they wanted was to defend their village if attacked, but no more. When they finally acted, it was too late to encircle the bandits. Few of the Machnovzy would have escaped had they been attacked by disciplined fighters. The truth is that as soon as the Machnovzy are out of the village, the Mennonites cease to shoot at them. They refuse to accept one of the basic principles of war: the fleeing enemy must be destroyed if at all possible.

Peter Braun too is in the forward line. They have just passed a peasant's home when a bandit comes out of the door. He had been in quest of loot and did not notice when his friends fled. There is nothing heroic about him; his gun hangs from the left shoulder and his arms are full of loot. When he finds himself surrounded by armed Mennonites consternation covers his face. A young Russian officer, one of several among the Mennonites, approaches the trembling man, revolver in hand.

"You dog! You dog!" he snarls as he lifts his to the fearful man's face.

Peter Braun grabs the officer's arm, "No!" he shouts, "We are not bandits! We do not shoot prisoners."

In rage the officer turns on Peter. "You…" but the words stick in his throat when he looks into Peter's blazing eyes. His eyes sweep the circle of men standing around him. What he reads in their eyes makes him lower his weapon.

"Alright." He says, "Have it your way. Send him to headquarters. Let them handle it. But this is a waste of time, fellows. We are fighting for keeps. We have no time for tender feelings." The man is led away.

The Halbstadt men spend the night in Sparau. The next day they return home, bringing the two dead with them. How many many dead the Machnovzy have lost is not known, but it is certainly more. The skirmish is the first battle experience of the *Selbstschutz***. From this day on the Machnovzy have a healthy respect for the Mennonite militia.

** The *Selbstschutz* (literally: self-defense) were units of armed Mennonites in southern Russia who tried t oprotect their villages from the attacking bandits.

A few days later John Martens and Sergeant Henschel are buried in the cemetery at Halbstadt. Very many people present at the funeral and most are deeply shaken.

CHAPTER NINETEEN

RESCUE OF BLUMENFELD

Just as most well-established Mennonite farmers, the Brauns had a second, smaller building in their yard. Usually such a building consisted of two rooms and a kitchen. When children married they often lived therefor a few years. Or when a farmer and his wife became old and handed the farm over to one of their children, they retired into this smaller house to spend the last years of their life there. The Brauns had such a house, though for some time it had not been occupied. In one room they kept old furniture and things of that nature and the second they used as a workshop. A farmer using wood or leather always had something to repair.

Now the house was once again occupied. Mrs. Braun had a married sister who had lived in Blumenfeld, about fifty miles away. The Johann Friesens had been successful farmers and once had a splendid farm. The day came, however, when they were forced to flee for their lives leaving all their worldly goods behind. From then on they lived in the small house on the Braun's farm. The events that had taken place in Blumenfeld were already wellknown to most of the Mennonite colonists.

In 1803 the Russian government, eager to populate the newly-acquired and empty stretches north of the Black Sea, had given the

Mennonite brotherhood a piece of virgin land comprising a block of 360,000 acres. In the years that followed additional settlers came and new villages sprang up; and in time the children of the settlers founded more villages until there were 57 of them and all the land granted to the brotherhood was occupied. To provide for their many offspring, most of whom became farmers, the mother colony bought wide stretches of virgin land from Russian estate owners to settle them on.

Thus in southern and eastern Russia many Mennonite daughter colonies came into existence.

Alongside this came another development. Individuals with the money bought land from Russian land owners and became estate owners themselves. Sometimes their holdings ran into thousands of acres, but there were also many small estates, perhaps 800 acres or so in size. In quite a number of cases several families together bought an estate and then established a small village. These villagers were well-to-do, each one owning possibly some 800 acres, and their fine buildings, excellent horses and pure-bred cattle bore witness to their wealth. The large Molotschna settlement was surrounded by such estates and small Mennonite villages were scattered among the Russian population. These Mennonites practically always got along well with their Russian neighbours, yet at the same time there remained a certain distance between the Russians and the Mennonites. The Mennonites were of a different nationality, spoke another language, did not belong to the Orthodox Church and were much better off than their Russian neighbours. The Russians found the differences practically impossible to overlook.

When the Revolution broke the estate owners and the settlers in the small villages surrounded by Russian neighbours were the first to feel the fury of unchained passions. Robberies, violence and murder were the order of the day. Those who could, fled, seeking safety in the larger Mennonite settlements, such as the Molotschna or the Old Colony. Many did not make it; they were murdered in their homes or on the road to safety.

East of the city of Orechov and 18 miles from Gulaj Pole (the home town of the bandit leader Nestor Machno), and about 50 miles from the Molotschna settlement, had stood since 1848 the small Mennonite village of Blumenfeld. It was well-to-do and a beautiful village. There were ten farmsteads in the village, a flour mill, a brick-making factory, a blacksmith shop, a fine school and a church.

By 1918 the estate owners of this area were being attacked, robbed and in many instances murdered. Those who could, fled. Bandits began to appear in Blumenfeld too, committing their familiar crimes. Between this village and the Molotschna lay the Lutheran village of Blumenthal, which became a gateway for the bandits to the German settlements on the Molotschna river. Many of the bandits were making their headquarters in the Russian village of Kopani from where they were attacking Blumenthal. The Selbstschutz men of that village, strongly supported by men from the Prishib, Halbstadt and Gnadenfeld volosts, kept the bandits in check. In the many skirmishes that were fought in this vicinity the bandits invariably got the worst of it. The result was a much more dangerous situation for the Blumenfeld settlers. Flight for them was impossible. On their way to the Molotschna they would have to pass through the large Russian village of Malo Takmachka. There was little hope that they could pass through it and live. The bandits who molested the settlement practically daily, taunted them, "You are hoping that your comrades from Halbstadt will show up here one day to rescue you. Don't wait. You won't see them because we shall slaughter all of you before they come!"

By January, 1919, the Blumenfeld people had a feeling that a climax was approaching. The bandits were getting more vicious all the time and something was bound to happen. People prayed fervently to God, their only hope. On January 19th the bandits seemed to be nervous. They had robbed and threatened but for the night left the village, promising to come back the next day. In the darkness of the evening the settlers sat in their homes behind locked doors not daring to light their lamps for fear that lights might attract the bandits. Schoolteacher Enns sat in his dark room and watched the street. Suddenly he saw a dozen to fifteen armed riders approach. His heart beat faster. The men turned into the school yard and began to beat against the door. With a sinking heart Enns went to open up when to his great joy he heard Low German sounds. Before him stood Selbstschutz men from the Molotschna, some of them men he knew personally. They told Enns that they had come to rescue the Blumenfeld villages. 300 mounted men had occupied Malo Tokmachka, they said. They had come to see what the situation in Blumenfeld was and whether the village could accompany all of them. They would remain there for the night. The villagers were getting ready to leave with them the next morning. Enns assured the men that they could be accommodated. They rode back to get their friends. The news was passed from house to house and the settlers began to prepare for their flight. Time went by but no riders showed up. The villagers began to hear artillery fire now, the village of Malo Tokmachka was being shelled. Then ten or twelve riders rode into the village. Their cavalry had retreated, they said, since they were being fired upon with artillery fire. If the villagers wanted to come with them, they had to be ready in half an hour. No time could be lost. One of the farmers complained that a public meeting would have to be called to discuss the situation. But the riders responded that there was nothing to be discussed. Those who wanted to come had to be ready in half an hour, for then the riders would be leaving. Thirty minutes later a long line of wagons and droshkeys loaded with villagers, young and old, well and sick, was ready on the street. Slowly the line began to move. The riders covered both sides. The night was dark. In Malo Tokmachka they saw no trace of the cavalry. No one spoke more than was absolutely necessary. They got safely through the large village. Twenty miles further, in the Russian village of Sladkaja Balka, the refugees met with the main company of riders. Now the spell was broken and people began to talk. Surrounded by 300 young armed riders, the long train continued and in the morning reached the first Mennonite Village. They were saved - more than 100 people. Yesterday they had been homeowners, today they were homeless. All they had possessed they had left behind. They had only about half an hour to pick up some of the things most dear to them. But they were very thankful. They were free from the inhuman terrors of the bandits. Their prayers had been answered. The Selbstschutz men seemed like saviours to them, men who had risked their lives for them.

The Johann Friesens and their two children, a grownup son and a teenage daughter, had come with two wagons and six good horses. They had loaded as much as possible on their wagons in half an hour and the two teams and what was on the wagons was all they carried away. They drove to Margenau to the Peter Brauns, their relatives. The Brauns received them with open arms and offered them their small house for a home. The Friesens thankfully accepted it.

CHAPTER TWENTY

FIGHTS AGAINST MACHNO'S BANDS

The die had been cast. To continue the fight the settlement needed weapons and ammunition. Two men, Epp and Krause, were delegated to get in touch with the White Army in the Crimea. The loyalist army heads received them sympathetically. The Mennonites came home with five carloads of arms and ammunition; four machine guns, field telephones, hand grenades and many other things needed by a fighting unit. Despite the help, the Selbstschutz remained poorly armed throughout its existence. There were too few machine guns, no artillery to speak of; for the most part the men had to rely on hand weapons only.

The White Army had suggested that Russian military officers lead the Mennonite fighting units and had offered a Russian colonel named Malakov, a Bulgarian by birth, to be in charge of the Selbstschutz. The situation by this time was chaotic. Russian officers had somehow established themselves in the Mennonite villages and taking advantage of the uncertain situation and being considered specialist in warfare, they manage to can considerable influence. These officers attempted to integrate the Selbstschutz with the White Army but this the Mennonites staunchly resisted. They felt it was undesirable to permit outsiders, men who really had very little in common with them, to control their situation. Instead a committee was elected to be in charge of all military matters, into which were elected or appointed the following men: a Neufeld from Schoensee; a Plett from Tiegerweide; a Friesen from Blumstein; a Schroeder from Halbstadt; a Rempel from Gnadenfeld; a Toews from Waldheim; a Warkentin from Waldheim; an Esau from Friedensruh; a Richert from Gnadenfel; and a J. Epp. Epp was elected chairman of the committee. All the elections or appointments were made by a relatively small section of the brotherhood. The Mennonites as a whole knew little about what was happening.

The committee met in Halbstadt to discuss the situation and invited a few well-known men to sit in with them. They wanted to separate the Selbstschutz from any Russian officers and the army administration. Colonel Malakov was invited to the meeting and informed about the thinking of the committee. A sharp exchange ensued until Malakov finally realized that the Mennonites meant business. They spelled out to him in no uncertain terms that they were not a regular military unit and that they did not wish to engage in any political actions. They wanted no more than to protect themselves from the bandits until a government would assert itself. They drew up the following document:

"We, the Mennonites of the Halbstadt and Gnadenfeld volosts, united, armed and organized as a Selbstschutz during times of stress when we were molested, subjected to burnings, robbed, rape and murdered by the various roaming bands. The Selbstschutz is no military organization capable of aggressive war, but was designed to protect our lives and possessions against robber bands. We Mennonites are no revolutionary party and we do not wish to exercise military power. If a permanent government emerges

in Russia, especially in the Ukraine, we solemnly declare that, regardless of its political persuasion, we will lay down all our arms and submit to this government."

The declaration was signed by all members of the committee and clearly communicated to the Russian officers. Copies were placed in the volost offices.

Peter Braun too had joined the Selbstschutz, though he had done so very reluctantly. By now he was 27 years old, had seen the war, and been through a great deal. He was too old for adventures. He also felt a deep revulsion to all force and was quite familiar with the Mennonite position regarding warfare. As a Christian he felt that he could not shoot at human beings. Yet at the same time he heard the terrible stories and saw the despair and hopelessness that hung like a pall over the faces of those who had fallen into the hands of the bandits. Could he allow this to happen to his mother and fine young sisters? He couldn't, and so Peter too joined the Selbstschutz.

He had participated in the skirmish in Tshernigovka. They had dislodged the bandits but Peter knew militarily speaking they had made a blunder by not destroying their retreating enemy. A deep-seated aversion to bloodshed had made the Selbstschutz unit cease shooting as soon as the bandits were out of the village. They had been allowed to retreat safely. Peter knew that the fellows whom they had spared would be back, quite possibly as their executioners. But what was the solution?

On one occasion a Lutheran village had been attacked. The village Selbstschutz, unable to keep the bandits out, had retreated taking all the villagers with them. Only the village herdsman with his sons remained. The family was sure that they had nothing to fear since they were very poor. A Mennonite unit, Peter among them, was ordered to clear the village of the invaders. They advanced in a line and there was some shooting. By now the Machnovzy had a healthy respect for the fighting power of the colonists. They retreated slowly. In a hedge the Selbstschutz surprised a young member of the Machnovzy. It was a peasant boy of no more than 18 years. When he faced the Selbstschutz men he was so surprised that, gun in hand, he took off his cap, bowed before them and said: "Good day, gentlemen! Good day!" A Russian officer rushed forward. "Just a minute. Keep your greeting for your father, the devil. You'll be with him in hell this very minute," and he raised his gun. But David Koop, a student, interfered: "Lieutenant, do not shoot! You should know by now that we do not murder prisoners." The Lieutenant looked at the other men and lowered his gun. Grumbling, he stepped aside and the prisoner was led away by one of the Mennonite men. They would never entrust a prisoner to a Russian; if they did, it was unlikely he would ever reach their headquarters.

They kept advancing. It so happened that Peter was the first to reach the herdsman's hut. The door stood widely ajar. Cautiously Peter entered. His heart nearly stopped beating and his senses wanted to refuse to register what he saw before his eyes. The four men, father and three sons, lay dead, fearfully mutilated. Their ears had been cut off and their eyes gouged out. These men had been poor labourers serving for wages. Why had this been done to them?

For a while Peter leaned against the wall. This is what he faced. He fought a constant inner battle about serving in the Selbstschutz and shooting at human beings. But were they human beings? What kind of humans would do such terrible things? What would these men, unresisted, do to his mother and sisters? *"Oh God! Oh God!"* he shouted aloud. *"I don't have the answer. I don't know. I don't want to sin. But I know that as long as I live I can't let this happen to innocent people. You be my righteous judge. You know and understand. I have no choice but to resist this band."*

He went out into the village street. The bandits had left, but what a sight! Dogs and farm animals lay wantonly shot to death. The doors of the houses stood open, many windows were broken. One house was burning. Things looted and then dropped, lay on the street. Several young Russian fellows were caught in the village still in the process of robbing. A number of them were shot, but not by the Mennonites. The latter consistently refused to shoot prisoners or unarmed individuals Several Russian women were also caught. When they were asked what they were doing in the village, they claimed that they had come to milk the cows. The owners had fled and the poor cows would be suffering. These women were stretched over a fence or bench and given a sound thrashing. With the advice not to come robbing again they were allowed to go home.

Peter knew the Russian officer who had wanted to shoot the prisoner. Later when he got the chance, he said to the man:

"May I ask you a question, please?" The man nodded and Peter continued: "You seem to be a refined man. You are an officer and not a bit rough, but when you had that poor misled peasant boy before you today you would have killed him had we not interfered. I cannot understand you. Why do you act the way you do?"

The officer was quiet for a while. It was obvious that he was very agitated. Then he related: "My parents had a small estate - not rich, but they were well-to-do. My sisters are married and have homes of their own. So there we were, my parents and I, living on our estate. We knew that times were dangerous, but where could we go? We remained on our estate. A few months ago I had left home for a few days. When I returned I noticed immediately that something terrible had happened. Our dogs lay dead on the yard and the door of the house stood open. Inside I found my father, grossly mutilated, dead on the floor. In my parent's bedroom I found my mother. She was unconscious and her face was badly battered. She had been beaten. I brought water, washed her face and revived her. In broken sentences she told me what had happened. Five armed strangers had come into the house. My parents were forced to feed the bandits; then they had gone into the barn, hitched the best team of horses to a wagon and driven up to the front door. They began to load up what appealed to them: bedding, clothing, dishes, anything they wanted. They demanded money of father and he gave them what little he had. They wanted more and began to beat him. Then they tied Father to the bed and the five took turns raping mother and beating her too. When they still were given no money, simply because my father had none, they killed Father and left. I did for Mother what I could. At night I slept some, but when I woke Mother was gone - I found her body in the well. She couldn't face life. I joined the White Army and since then I haven't taken prisoners. I have shot them!"

Peter was quiet for a while and then he asked "But is that the solution?" The Russian too was silent for a moment and then he replied: "It is not. I know it is not. But there is no solution that I know of. The Whites are going to lose this struggle because too few among them want to create a new and better world. Most of them want only to set the clock back so that things will remain more or less as they have always been. But that is impossible. The Reds have proclaimed a class war. They consider men like me their enemies and say openly that we must be eliminated. There is no future for us. The world that we know is dying and we must die with it. Sooner or later a bullet will get me too. I am waiting for it. I long for the peace that only Mother Earth can give to those who've been laid to rest in her bosom." "Do .you believe in the existence of God?" Peter asked. "I do," replied the lieutenant, "and

I see him as the understanding, compassionate and just one. He knows that many like me have been driven into a blind alley; that we torture ourselves and cannot find a way out of our predicament. During the war we were forced to shed blood. We were told that the Germans were evil. But now our own people behave far worse than any foreign enemy has ever done. If it was right for us to fight the Germans, how much more cause do we have to fight the men who destroy all that we hold sacred."

The Lutheran village of Blumenthal, situated about 30 miles north of the Molotchna centre of Halbstadt, was strategically situated and controlled the approach to the three German volosts of Gnadenfeld, Halbstadt and Prishib. Here Mennonites, Lutherans and Catholics united in a common cause and fought side by side to keep the bandits out of their villages. The nearby Russian village of Kopani was used by the Machnovzy as a base from which to operate against the German settlers. The local Selbstschutz was too weak to keep these bandits at bay and thus units from other places were practically continuously stationed in Blumenthal. These were fed by the local settlers which was no longer a simple matter. However the villagers, who were mortally afraid of the bandits, were glad to have help stationed in their village whatever the cost.

The defenders had thrown an earthen wall around the village and from behind its protection they shot at the approaching enemies. Before them lay a wide and open field which the Machnovzy had to cross to get at the defenders. Many skirmishes were fought here and the Machnovzy were thrown back every time. The defenders, inexperienced as they were in military matters, made mistakes too. On one occasion three local boys were ordered to find out if there were bandits in Kopani. They rode fearlessly into the village and suddenly found themselves surrounded. Two were able to escape, but the third was killed. The bandits followed with a determined attack lasting from morning till night. They formed a line and a commissar rode in front of the line on a beautiful horse encouraging and instructing his men. The distance from the wall was such that he must have felt safe, but among the colonists were some excellent shots. One of them sent the rider tumbling from his horse. In his fright he came running right up to the wall and was taken by the Selbstschutz as a prisoner of war.

Early in March, 1919, the Selbstschutz made its last stand in Blumenthal. The Whites had retreated and Machno had allied himself with the Red forces. But this was not known to the Mennonite colonists. About four hundred men from various Mennonite villages and another two hundred students of the Kommerzschule were at this time in Blumenthal. They were confronted by about three thousand Machnovzy. By now these bands were much better armed than the settlers. Machno had six machine guns and three big cannons. He had put the machine guns on droshkies pulled by teams of three horses. These droshkies were very maneuverable. The coachman could swing his horses in any direction and then face and fire the gun in the opposite direction. The Machno men advanced along a long line and at intervals moved the droshkies. The defenders concentrated their fire on these horses. When these fell the machine gun was immobilized. For the rest they held their fire until the attackers were quite close and then with concentrated and well-directed shots cut the Machnovzy down. The line wavered, and then turned and ran. This was repeated every time the Machnovzy mounted an attack. Finally the field in front of the wall was covered with the wounded and dead.

Peter Braun with two other men were stationed in the home of a Lutheran farmer by the name of Scheffler. The couple were approaching their 60s. There were two sons in the home, one 27 and the other 24 years old. There were more children but these were married and on their own. The home and the yard bore quiet evidence that the family were good farmers and had once been well-to-do. Peter and his two companions were treated royally. Yet time had effected everybody in this home.

The parents were bewildered. They could not understand what was happening. All their lives they had worked hard and tried to live irreproachably and then the tragic war of 1914 had come. Suddenly the papers began saying nasty things about them. The government planned to dispossess them and ban them to the inhospitable north. Nevertheless, their two sons were mobilized into the army to defend the fatherland. Their oldest son had fallen on the Turkish front and was buried on Turkish soil. The parents grieved for their firstborn.

The second son too had been in the army, was wounded and then came home.

Then the bandits descended upon them. They had been robbed and beaten and threatened with death And now their sons were out there defending the village and their home and again risking their lives. These boys should have married and had homes of their own by now. But as things were, there was no time for such matters. Life had become a hopeless maze and the future looked dark. How would it all end?

That was the question Peter Braun and his company were asking too: *"How was this all going to end?"*

They didn't have long to wait for an answer. One day artillery shots from big cannons began pouring into Blumenthal. Whole houses were blown to pieces. The two small cannons of the defenders were silenced. Then a line began to move towards the wall. In consternation the defenders realized that this was no longer the rabble they had been dealing with. These were regular and well-trained fighters. It was the Red Army which had made common cause with Machno. Thousands of soldiers confronted the colonists.

The villagers realized that their situation was desperate. Flight was impossible, surrender unthinkable. Commands were no longer needed, each man did all he could and more. With deadly accuracy they shot their rifles and machine guns as fast as they could. Many attackers dropped to the ground, yet still the line held and drew closer. Already the men could see the shining buttons on the soldiers' uniforms. Then the line wavered, held momentarily, and then turned and ran. For the moment the village was safe.

Heavy artillery fire now racked Blumenthal and its defenders. Towards evening the human line appeared again. Slowly it moved toward the wall. It halted and the men began to prepare for the night. A human chain had encerciled the village. Escape seemed impossible; in the morning the final hour of reckoning would likely come. Lips drawn tight with fear whispered many a prayer.

The Selbstschutz had twenty-five mounted men in the village. The night was dark. Quietly the men on horses lined up on the western end of the village. Each man was given a number of hand grenades. Wagons filled with men lined up behind the riders. On some of them machine guns were mounted so that they could shoot to the right and to the left. At a given signal the mounted men rushed forward, throwing grenades among the Red Army men. The wagons that followed fired to both sides. A panic ensued among the encircling soldiers and the defenders broke through the ring without any loss of life. A few were wounded, not by their opponents but by shrapnel from the grenades thrown by their friends.

The fleeing men, pursued by their enemy, reached the Lutheran village of Tiefenbrun. Here they again readied themselves for the defense. The Reds encircled the village and set up their artillery. It was obvious that the next morning the village would be shelled and a final attack launched. Escape seemed to be impossible. But again a way out was found. A local man informed the defenders that on one side of the village stood a brick burning factory. For many years it had used the blue clay that could be found underground here and in time a tunnel leading from the factory to a valley outside the village had been dug. The tunnel was high and wide enough for a team to drive through. The citizen said that he could lead all the Selbstschutz men and the villagers to safety. During the night every living being was evacuated from the village and fled. Early in the morning the Reds opened with artillery fire upon the village, setting the houses aflame and demolishing most of them. Then they marched against the village. To their surprise they found no dead and no defenders either. The village was empty. The attackers were dumbfounded.

Meanwhile the Selbstschutz had reached Waldek. This village is a natural fortress and here they had a chance to keep their attackers at bay for some time. The Reds who were following them realized by now that the conquest of the village would be costly. They sent four negotiators who were to offer the Selbstschutz men free passage to their homes provided that they would lay down their weapons and make a solemn promise to cease all resistance against the Red Army. But the Mennonites never heard the offer. The four White officers who met with the opposite side's negotiators killed the men and buried their bodies. The Reds again opened fire. The night following, a very dark night, the Mennonites who knew the area well were able to escape again. They gave up all attempts at continuing an unequal fight and scattered into their villages. The Selbstschutz as an organization had ceased to exist.

CHAPTER TWENTY-ONE

SURRENDER AND EVALUATION

Elsewhere representatives of the Mennonites had gone to meet the commanders of the Red forces. They took the resolution drawn up in Halbstadt earlier which clarified their position, and presented it to the commanding general in an appeal for pardon for the bloodshed that had occurred. To their relief the explanation was accepted and a pardon promised to the men provided they would lay down their weapons within three days. The condition was also accepted and announcements to that effect were sent to all the villages. Most of the Selbstschutz men willingly complied, except some who did not trust the promise and fled with the retreating Whites to the Crimea.

The large village of Gnadenfeld was a cultural, religious and administrative centre. During these days it was crowded with former Selbstschutz men. Russians and fleeing White Army soldiers. All were afraid of the things to come. The volost office was usually crowded with humanity.

One day the elder of the Pordenau Mennonite church, Peter Epp, entered the building. With flashing eyes he shouted loudly: "Brethren, we have sinned. We neglected to trust in the Lord and instead trusted in our own strength. For us there is but one way. We must confess our sins and turn to the Lord for mercy. Let us pray!"

With these words, Epp kneeled down where he stood. All men present, Mennonites and Russians, knelt with him. Epp prayed loudly. It was a confession and a prayer for mercy. Then he stood up and turned to his son, the former chairman of the defense committee, who had obtained weapons from the Whites, and said to him, "Son, the war is over. Let us go home!" and with that the two left the room.

Peter Braun spent the last two days before the collapse of the Selbstschutz in Halbstadt, staying with his relatives there. But whenever possible he was at the teacher Janzen's home. He heard about more of the outrages the Machnovzy had perpetrated in regions they had occupied. He was told of several instances in Mennonite homes where the bandits, after being fed and provided with all that the family was able to offer, robbed the home and then tied the husband to the bed and gang-raped his wife before his eyes. Anyone who interfered was tortured and murdered. He heard of a Wilhelm Janzen who had come to the assistance of his sister and was cut to pieces. On the other hand, occasionally interference did help, as happened in the case of an estate-owning Peters family.

A bandit with a drawn sword stood before Anna Bahnmann. She was to submit to him or die. Her stepfather Peters came into the room. The bandit ordered him out but the man refused. The bandit lifted his sword and the Mennonite jumped at him. He shouted, "Anna, run and hide yourself." Then with his bare hands he got hold of the sword. The bandit pulled and eventually pulled it out of the man's hands cutting them fearfully. Again he lifted the sword, and once more the father got hold of it and again after a struggle it was pulled through his hands. Then the man was able to give the attacker a heavy push, free himself and run out of the room. He escaped and so did the girl. The father lived, but his hands were so mutilated that he would never again be able to use his fingers.

Peter wanted very badly to discuss the Selbstschutz with Janzen. "Was it a tactical mistake for the Mennonites of the Molotschna region to defend themselves against the Machno hordes?" he asked the teacher philosopher.

Janzen replied carefully, "That is a very difficult question to answer. Before we attempt to do so there is another question that we must try to find an answer to. Namely, is an individual who is faced with annihilation never allowed to defend himself? Or is it right to seek protection from armed police or guards? And is there a difference between the two?

"Our idea was and is non-violence. But we live in a world of realities and realities never catch up with that ideal. What we believe should be done and what life allows us to do are often far apart. When we are really put to the task, as in the Terek region or in the Amur-Darja incident of the 1880s, total non-resistance simply proves to be untenable. That is the reason our villages reached for weapons. It can be argued that the Molotschna people are too unspiritual and that their lack of spirituality caused their downfall; if that is so, we admit our shortcomings. But the Mennonites of the last century were a select group and very serious. They had given up their homes and all their worldly possessions for their faith. They were as close to perfection as a group of believers can be, and yet, when absolutely no human help could be expected from anywhere, and degradation and death stared them in the face, they reached for their guns and defended themselves. We too have done this.

Would we have suffered less if we had not resorted to force and had patiently submitted to those who murdered and molested us? No one can answer such a question with assurance. All of us are only expressing opinions. Some of our leaders, such as the respected B. B. Janz, have answered yes to this question. We would have suffered either way, but less had we not offered resistance, they say. Then God would have protected us.

"Other, equally respected men, feel much differently. If the Selbstschutz had not kept the bandits at bay for some six months until the Red Army arrived, they believe even more terrible things would have happened. There are many instances of horrible outrages perpetrated without any provocation whatsoever. In all their skirmishes the Selbstschutz lost four men, a surprisingly small number. Many believe that God has protected us through the Selbstschutz. No one can say for sure who is right and who is wrong, but the great majority of our people sincerely believe that the Selbstschutz literally saved us from annihilation."

"Was it a failure from a Christian point of view protect ourselves as we have been doing?" asked Peter.

Janzen pondered again and then responded, "This too will be answered in various ways. Some will say 'Unquestionably' while others - and this is the great majority - feel that there are moments in life when self defense is justified, and protection of others may be required of us. We will likely always have these diverse views. They have existed since the time of Christ and likely will continue to exist to the end of time.

"Our young men in the defense units on the whole behaved well. They avoided violence and bloodshed as much as they could. There were individuals who became intoxicated by the guns in their hands and sinned, but they were a small minority. I think that our people, who were only 'earthen vessels,' could not have acted much differently at a time when there was no protection anywhere and evil bands threatened not only their possessions and life but sadistically tortured and gang-raped their mothers, wives and sisters. It was this wholesale attack upon our women which likely was the strongest motive for the Selbstschutz."

But not only evil deeds were done during the dark days without government. The Janzens related a noble, sacrificial act that had taken place in Halbstadt just before the organization of the Selbstschutz. In Halbstadt lived two Sudermann brothers, identical twins who could only with difficulty be told apart. One of them was married and a father with children, the other a bachelor.

One day both were arrested. Some years before one of them had given a Russian a beating. This man was now one of a raiding band and wanted his revenge. He could not tell which of the two brothers had beaten him and so both were put in jail. The guilty one was to confess or both would have to die. It turned out that the married brother was the one who had thrashed the fellow. He knew that he would have to give himself up, but his brother convinced him not to. This one argued that since his brother had a wife and children he owed it to them to save bis life. As a bachelor, he would not be missed too much, he would offer himself to the bandits. He did, and his brother, the guilty one, remained free and alive. The body of the man who voluntarily gave his life to save a husband and father, was found some distance from the town.

Whenever Peter struggled with the question of the rightness or wrongness of the Selbstschutz, among other horrible scenes there came to his mind a fine young Mennonite boy. In his mind he heard him say as he had said to Peter's face, "Repeatedly the bandits came to our home. They robbed us, they beat our father, my brother and me, but we did not try to resist. Then one day two men came to our home and tried to take our mother. My brother and I killed them." His face twisted as he went on: "No one can molest my mother as long as I am alive and can do something about it." At such moments Peter's heart filled with compassion. The boy quite obviously was suffering, but given the same situation he would do again what he had done.

Peter had to say good-bye to his pleasant friends, the Janzens. They had enriched his life. He was departing from Halbstadt and he had no assurance that he would ever see these people again. Mrs. Janzen held Peter's hand and with feeling said, "May the Lord go with you." Peter turned quickly and left the home.

CHAPTER TWENTY-TWO

FLIGHT TO THE CRIMEA

During the last few months of the Selbstschutz Peter Braun had served in the cavalry. The day the Selbstschutz fled from Waldeck he was in Halbstadt. There he was informed that the front was shattered. Fleeing Selbstschutz men were coming through the town in great numbers. They disposed of their weapons in the yard of the volost office and continued their flight.

Peter had to make a decision - return to his village or flee to the Crimea. Some hoped at that time that the Whites would be able to maintain themselves on this natural fortress. Although the Reds had promised not to prosecute the men who had fought in the Selbstschutz, Peter, along with others, did not trust the promise. He was afraid to fall into Red hands and decided to flee to the Crimea. He walked to the place where his horse was quartered. As he went a group of about 60 unarmed labourers with Red flags came in the opposite direction. They were on their way to the volost office which they intended to take under their control. They sympathised with the Bolsheviks but not with the Machno bands. Peter, with gun over his shoulder and revolver at his side, had to pass the group. They let him pass without an unpleasant word.

He took his horse and rode to Petershagen. There he said goodbye to several relatives and then continued his flight via Melitopol to the Crimea. By now he was joined by seventeen other riders and a droshky with four German officers on it. All were seeking a place of refuge. For the night they stopped in an empty home whose owner too had fled. The next day they overtook a wanderer with a pack on his shoulders whom they recognized as the Lutheran pastor from the large village of Prishib. He too was fleeing. Since he had no horses and since his parishioners had been too preoccupied with themselves, he had no alternative but to walk.

"Reverend," the Selbstschutz men inquired, "have your parishioners not offered you a ride or some means of transportation?"

"No," answered the clergyman. "They needed every corner of their wagons to transport their own goods. They wouldn't be bothered with me."

The officers offered the man a seat in their droshky which he gratefully accepted. On the second day of their flight the group arrived in Spat in upper Crimea. Here they rested for two days before continuing their flight. All except Peter Braun and another man, who remained with friends in Spat, continued on.

The two Mennonite villages, Spat and Menlertschick, were close to the railway station Sarabus. Spat was a cultural and industrial centre, a large and beautiful village with many trees. A Mennonite family took Peter Braun into their home and gave him free lodging and meals, but Peter's horse had to work for his own and his master's keep. Here the two Selbstschutz men lived peacefully for a few weeks, and then on a Sunday they paid a visit to the village of Menlertschick. This was a small but lovely and wealthy village. Crop failures were unknown in this region and fruit trees grew beautifully. By now many refugees were living in Menlertschick, mostly estate owners from the Molotschna area. Peter found young and old acquaintances there, some of them related to him. He immediately decided to move there too. A local family agreed to take him in. He could stay at their home without any charge as long as he wanted to. Since by now Peter was bare of all worldly goods except his good horse, the free room was very important to him. Some of these people had fled from the Molotschna much later than Peter and they could give him some information about what had happened after his flight.

Although the Reds had promised that there would be no St. Bartholomew's Day massacre after they took over, everybody knew the situation was very grave. The villages sat on a powder keg capable of exploding at any time. Some of the Mennonite villages were by now occupied by forces of the Red Army but the greater number by those of the dreaded Machno units. These bandits said openly that they would like nothing better than to slaughter all Germans, but for the time being they were inhibited from doing so. They searched for hidden weapons and seemed to suspect that they would find them in chests of drawers and wardrobes. Many a cherished family treasure found its way into the pockets of these fighters for freedom, as they liked to style themselves.

Machno himself had his headquarters in the home of a Kliewer family in the village of Waldheim. Kliewer was a former estate owner and naturally feared for his life, but Machno assured him that he had nothing to fear from him. Nothing happened to Kliewer as long as Machno was in his home. Then one day he left. As soon as he was gone his followers cornered Kliewer and took him with them. They were on horseback and Kliewer was forced to run alongside one of the riders. Then they beat him to death and his mutilated body was found in the steppe. A totally innocent young man from Hierschau was killed by the bandits.

After a time the *Cheka* appeared. This was a court with extraordinary rights, in reality a group of sadists who in the name of social justice could do as they pleased with any human being. The members of the Cheka were total strangers and representatives of various national groups, gypsies among them. This news depressed Peter and he lay awake nights thinking about it. What might be happening at home now? What about his parents and his brothers and sisters? What about his friends? For months there was no news from the Molotschna.

The siege of the Crimea by the Red Army had broken all communication with the outside. The uncertainty was hard on the fugitives. The news from the front was not good and it was feared that the Reds would soon occupy the Crimea or at least part of it. What would happen to the former Selbstschutz men? Anyone who knew the Reds was convinced that sooner or later these men would be arrested. What would happen to them then was anyone's guess.

A German officer named Homeyer, who had been commanding the Selbstschutz during the last weeks of it's existence, now came forward with an unusual plan. He invited the former defenders to join a cavalry brigade he was organizing. This brigade would offer its services to the Reds to do garrison duty in the Crimea. If the Reds accepted the offer - and Homeyer thought they would - then the men were safe. They would then have become members of the Red Army and be free from persecution. The plan sounded somewhat fantastic, but since no one had a better idea and since the men scattered throughout the villages were afraid of the Reds, they volunteered for the *Jaegerbrigade* (rifle brigade) in Simferopol. Several thousand Germans joined Homeyer's organization, the majority Catholics and Lutherans though there were also a good number of Mennonites among them. These formations occupied the military barracks in Simferopol and were well armed and supplied. When after some time the Reds entered the Crimea they accepted Homeyer's offer. For the time being these Germans were to garrison the city of Simferopol. Soon it became evident that the Reds did not trust them and before long the Jaegerbrigade had to surrender all their weapons. As a compromise each man was given a certificate of trustworthiness and allowed to go free. But the men knew that these certificates meant little and one day they would no longer protect them.

A lesson these German soldiers had learned in their service with the Reds was that not all Germans could be trusted either. Some of them, they knew, had served as secret spies for the Reds. But none of the known or suspected spies were Mennonites.

In June of 1919 the Whites attacked again. They pushed the Reds out of the Crimea and drove them south north past the city of Kursk. The south of Russia, including the Molotschna, was for a few months free from the Reds. Peter Brain and others who had fled south soon returned home. When in the fall of 1919 the Whites again began to retreat, Peter went with them. He did so because he was afraid to remain. He and many others feared that the Reds would eventually exterminate all former Selbstshutz men. They felt safer in the White Army.

Peter was now with a cavalry unit on the front. Very often he and his comrades had to go reconnoitering. A detachment of about fifteen men rode into the no-man 's territory between the opposing armies. When two such groups met, there would be a fight or - even better - each group tried to waylay the other. For a time Peter and his detachment had to ride 25 miles and back on one day to a White unit and make the foray every second day. The next day another group had to do the same thing. Their way led along the Dnjeper river and past a certain farmhouse. One day an elderly man met them and told them that a group of Reds had crossed the Dnjeper during the night and had occupied the farmhouse and set up several machine guns. They were waiting for the riders. If the men had not been warned most of them and possibly all would have been masacred. This time they took a detour, and so again arrived safely home. The Reds had been waiting for them. When they realized that the Whites would not come they were puzzled. "Why?" they asked. "They travel this road every single day and today they do not show up. What made them choose another road?" Finally they collected their weapons and as soon as it was dark crossed to the other side of the Dnjeper River. On another occasion the Whites occupied a large village and were attacked by a very large Red force.

These were Red soldiers who had been on the Polish front, but since the peace with Poland had been transferred to the south of Russia. The German brigade was assigned to one section of the village. The fight between the two armies had lasted some time when Peter and a few other men were sent to their headquarters with a message. When they arrived at the place they found the building deserted, empty. The Whites had retreated without even notifying the brigade. The village was filling up with Red cavalry belonging to the dreaded *Budyennovzy**.

Peter and his friends rode back. On the way they encountered riders. "Who are you?" they asked. "Budyennovzy!" was the reply. That meant that their brigade was cut off and in mortal danger. They had to be informed of their situation as soon as possible. Peter and his men spurred on their horses. A local citizen recognized them: "Those are Whites!" he yelled. "Kill them! Cut them to

---

* The *Budyennovzy* were Red Army calvary named after their leader, Seemen Budyenny, commander of the First Calvary Army in their war against Anton Denikin and Pyotr Wrange, military leaders of the White Army in South Russia.

pieces!" But the men reached their unit and warned the men of the danger. They began to withdraw immediately, but the unit would have been lost if it had not been for a man named Penner and several other men. These men calmly set up their machine guns and held the advancing Reds in check. Though some of the men were taken prisoners, most of the brigade escaped. Had it not been for Penner and his group, none would have gotten away. Finally, even the small group of machine gunners escaped. Penner was given the rank of an officer and promised the cross of St. George, one of the highest decorations in the Czarist army.

Slowly and relentlessly the Whites were pushed back. For weeks Peter Braun and his friends slept in their clothes. They had to be ready at a moment's notice to defend themselves or flee. It was very hard on the men. But in the end all was lost. Ships were waiting in the harbours to take to safety in foreign countries those that wanted to leave the country. A number of Mennonites boarded too and eventually landed in the U.S.A. They became known as the "Sixty-Two," because there were 62 of them in the group. Peter Braun, however, decided to remain in Russia. He rode back to Menlertschick to his old friends, obtained civilian clothing and pretended to have been a team driver forced into service by the Red Army.

When the Red front had passed Manlertschick Peter and three of his friends decided to venture the trip to the Molotschna settlement. They obtained a wagon and two rather poor horses. With them, on the wagon, they had among other things two pairs of harnesses. When they were asked, as they often were, their story was that they "were farmers from the Molotschna settlement who had been pressed to serve with their teams in the army. In the Crimea some of their horses had died and some had simply been appropriated by soldiers who needed them."

"There are the harnesses on the wagon, all we have left," they said. "We are on our way home."

To come up with such a story was not a simple matter. They could be asked with which unit they had been serving, when and where, and their answers had to coincide with the facts or they would be found out. The group of four was stopped often and just as often told their story. But they were always allowed to continue their journey. They were nearing the border of the peninsula when a Russian sentry stopped them. He seemed to be a determined man. When they gave their usual answer, he retorted, "Lies! Nothing but lies! You are quite obviously White officers who are trying to flee from your just punishment. You will have to come with me!" He began to search their wagon. In it he found a few personal things that appealed to him and he took possession of them.

At that Peter Braun stepped up to the man, looked him straight in the face and said: "Look here, mister! You have insulted us with your mistrust, and you have searched us and taken some of our things for yourself. You seem to have forgotten that we now have a just government and that any citizen can complain to it and get his rights. Let's go and find out. We have served the army for weeks, have lost our teams, and now we are getting such treatment? Let's go to the authorities and we will see who will have reason to be sorry, you or we. Let's go." The man looked at the four travellers and then threw the things he had already taken as his own back onto the wagon and said, "Go to the devil! Get out of here as fast as you can!" The men did not wait for a second invitation and drove off as fast as their poor horses could go.

CHAPTER TWENTY-THREE

PETER'S DEATH

Peter came home. He found his father had aged very much and spoke little. The world he had known and understood was gone. He felt lost.

Peter's mother was gone. She had been ill for many months, but more likely she had died of a broken heart. She had been unable to cope with what had happened to them. Her oldest son, Peter, was gone and Jakob would come home no more. Yes, she had her daughters, but even so, life had demanded too much of her. She could not take it. "Give my love to my sons," she had said. "Tell them I have longed for them day and night. My heart cannot stand the burden any longer. I must go." And so she was buried. It wasn't thought strange that someone should die of sorrow. Death seemed to have lost its bitterness for it promised peace from all fear and uncertainty.

Peter's sister Kathe was engaged to be married to Henry Penner. Life goes on under even the most trying conditions. Anna, his youngest sister, had grown up too. Happily, both girls had been spared the brutalities so many fine girls had been subjected to by heartless men.

The farmyard looked neglected. Things that should have been repaired had not. The barn seemed toe be empty. Where once twelve or fourteen horses had stood, four poor creatures now were standing. For several years the passing armies, whether they were Reds or the Whites, had been taking horses that appealed to them. In their place they left the farmer a few worn out beasts. Previously they had five or six milk cows and a number of young cattle. Now two cows and a single calf were all that was left to them. Some of their wagons had disappeared and the droshky had vanished.

The Whites had returned several times and occupied the Molotschna villages only to be pushed back time after time.

On November 10, 1919, a tragedy had occurred in the village of Blumenort. The Machno bandits had set up their headquarters in the village of Orloff in the home of the Goossen family. Here they caroused and from here they oppressed the surrounding villages. But so far they had neither killed people nor molested women. A number of young Mennonites, members of the White Army, and hidden in the villages, decided to liquidate this nest of oppression. On several wagons they drove to the village of Blumenort not far from Orloff. From here they planned to walk to Orloff. In Blumenort they drove into the yard of a well-known Mennonite by the name of Regehr. This man had a very large shed and the soldiers wanted to hide their teams in this shed. When Regehr saw them he was terrified. "Men," he said, "what do you intend to do? What do you want here? You will bring great misfortune over all of us. Please turn around and leave my yard. Leave us alone!"

In spite of the owner's protest and against his will the men drove their team into the shed and closed the large doors. From here they planned to walk to Orloff. At that moment there was a commotion on the street. A droshky loaded with bandits and accompanied by several riders had appeared in the village. The bandits were dragging a young Mennonite towards the droshky in order to take him with them. His sister was loudly calling for help. To the Whites the sudden appearance of the bandits came as a surprise and they began to shoot. Several of the bandits were hit but two riders escaped. The Whites now jumped on their wagons and fled to the village of Tiegerweide, leaving the citizens of Blumenort to their fate.

Early the next morning Machno cavalry entered the village. In their eyes the whole village was responsible for what happened. They arrested Regehr and his two sons, a teacher named Schmidt, a minister named Sudermann and several others and stuck them into a cellar. After a few hours they threw hand grenades into the cellar and slaughtered those who survived. Other men were murdered in their homes or yards. Altogether twenty men were killed. The next day they killed eleven men in the nearby village of Altonau and six in Orloff. Among the latter six was the student Johann Cornies, the last male descendent of Johann Cornies, the great Mennonite educator and model farmer.

For the first ten months of 1920 the front repeatedly passed over the Mennonite villages. Homes and yards were constantly filled with men of one party or the other. Death, rape and robbery were the order of the day. What was done to the girls and women during those months defies all description. In October the Whites were again and this time permanently dislodged from the area. From then on the Bolsheviks were in control. Few horses and cows survived. No grain was left in the bins and the homes were robbed empty. Contagious diseases had been brought into the villages, among them the dreaded typhus fever. Hundreds of citizens fell prey to the deadly disease and whole families were wiped out. The fields had not been worked since the horses had been taken and the cultivators of the soil assaulted. The summer of 1921 was very dry and the result was a famine. The famine eventually spread over all Russia and it was believed that about six million citizens of the stricken country died of starvation. The dead lay along the roadsides and on the streets of the villages and cities. Peter was told that 326 persons had died in the Molotschna villages. In the adjoining German volost of Prishib, out of a total population of 11,000, no less than 1,000 starved to death. Peter learned the fate of each person in Margenau. Many had passed away, some by illness, others by violent death. Still others had fled to some unknown place. Peter listened to the stories and felt as though he was past responding. It seemed as though all he felt was a great loneliness and exhaustion. He could see no future and no hope no matter how he looked at it. He recalled his friends, cut down by bullets or a sword. They were buried and slept in peace. Peter struggled against the feeling but could not help but envy the peaceful sleepers. He busied himself in the yard and in the garden; he wanted to forget and find his equilibrium.

One day armed men rode into the Braun's yard and asked for Peter. They spoke roughly and took Peter and several other young men with them. In Halbstadt they put the young Mennonites into a private home now serving as a jail. Altogether more than 80 persons, mostly young men but also a few girls, were arrested. They were accused of having formed a secret organization aimed at the overthrow of the new government. It was a ridiculous accusation and without a shred of truth. The prisoners were transported to Melitopol and lodged in jail there. It was a place of terror. Practically every night they were questioned, sometimes hours at a time. After two or three months the majority were set free, but the former Selbstschutz men were retained. They were transferred to a jail in Alexandrovsk, now called Zaporoshye. Here the questioning continued. It was like living in a lion's den.

The young men knew that any night could be their last one and they prepared for their departure. They sang a great deal. Songs they had learned in the village schools became very precious to them. They especially loved to sing, *"Nimm Jesu meine Haende"* (Take Thou my Hand, O Father), "Nearer my God to Thee" and *"Wenn ich einmal soll scheiden, dann scheide nicht von mir"* (When I depart this life, depart thou not from me). Someone among them had a Bible and practically daily, towards evening, they would read together a passage such as Psalm 121:

"I lift up my eyes to the hills.
From where does my help come?
My help comes from the Lord,
who made heaven and earth...
The Lord will keep you from all evil;
he will keep your life.
The Lord will keep
your going out and your coming in
from this time forth and forevermore."

Late one evening the door of the room opened. A young commissar, followed by armed men, stood in the door. In his hand he held a list. "Peter Braun, take your things and come with us!" he said. Peter gathered up his few belongings. Then he turned to his friends and said, "If any of you should remain alive, please give my love to my family, and especially to my old father. Tell them that I was ready. Death has no terrors for me. Good-bye, my friends." Then he left with the men. After a short while a shot was heard. Several other men were called in a similar way. "Give my love to my mother or my parents," they said, "Tell them I am at peace and ready." It is a great privilege to be brought up in a home where the Word of God is known and respected. It is a great blessing especially when it comes to dying.

The next morning when the remaining Mennonites were led from their cell for their daily walk in the prison yard, one of the guards asked them, with a mixture of curiosity and awe, "What was it about your comrades last night? What kind of people are you? These fellows didn't weep nor did they beg for their lives. It is very unpleasant to shoot such men." The men who remained were given several years in a prison labour camp. Before them as before millions of others loomed in gigantic letters the question:

"Why? What is the sense of all this?"

Other titles from **Schleitheim Press**:

And If I Don't?:
Reimagining the Single Life

By April Klassen

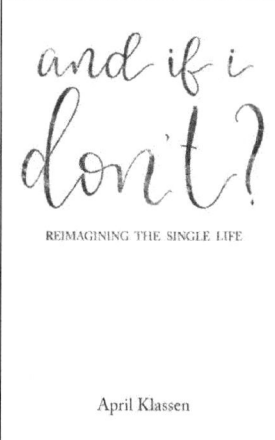

ISBN: 978-1-990389-00-9

In this book April Klassen outlines a biblical understanding of singleness within an evangelical framework. This non-fiction work is inspired by the author's own experiences with expectations of singleness and marriage in the contemporary church. The book describes the overlooked benefits of singleness in the church community. Ultimately, it advocates for Christians of all relationship statuses to pursue Christ wholeheartedly.

Life with God:
An Unexpected Encounter with God and the Supernatural Life that Followed

By Jordan Chanin

ISBN: 978-1-990389-03-0

Growing up without faith, Jordan Chanin's life was a pursuit of partying, sex and the next drug high. After an encounter with God during the throes of a family tragedy, he underwent a radical life transformation. In this original, biographical publication by Schleitheim Press, witness the miraculous impact that comes from devoted Christian life. Through this book be inspired to begin your own supernatural journey with God!

Learn more at **SchleitheimPress.com**

About Schleitheim Press

In 1527, in a small Swiss town near the border of Germany, Michael Sattler and a group of believers gathered to write the *Schleitheim Confession*, the first recorded statement of faith in what would become the Anabaptist movement. Many of those who signed the article were martyred in the days and months which followed. From this sincere and passionate group came a rich Christian tradition which has impacted churches of all denominations around the globe. *We seek to continue the legacy today and center our work around three of their core values.*

Anabaptist Core Value #1 – Applicable

First and foremost, we promise you that every book that we produce will be applicable. The books that we publish are not simply introducing theological concepts or ideas, far away from the reality of every day life. Instead, they are a written testimony. Of the goodness of God throughout lives, throughout generations, and throughout countless years. God *was* good, *is* good, and *will* be good to us. Forever and always.

Anabaptist Core Value #2 – Accessible

The Anabaptist movement stems from a desire to get God's word into the hands of laymen, and the second value Schleitheim Press stands for is accessibility. Our primary focus is on *you*, the readers, not profit. We are passionate about what we publish – we want people to be able to read our books, and don't want finances to be a barrier to access.

Anabaptist Core Value #3 – Affecting

Finally, we want our books to drive action - positive change in the world. As Anabaptists we look beyond ourselves and at the broader community. For us, that means that more than simply impacting the reader we also want to effect the wider community and world that we live in.

Learn more at *SchleitheimPress.com*

Printed by BoD"in Norderstedt, Germany